D1247901

THE LONELY SIDE OF THE RIVER

BY DONALD MacKENZIE

THE
LONELY SIDE
OF THE
RIVER

DONALD MacKENZIE

HOUGHTON MIFFLIN COMPANY BOSTON
THE RIVERSIDE PRESS CAMBRIDGE

For Ida

THE LONELY SIDE OF THE RIVER

Stephen Venner — Monday 29 June 1964

H<small>E</small> anchored his elbow on the leather-topped desk, holding the office phone steady. His quiet voice betrayed none of the violent alarm in his brain.

"Mr. and Mrs. Annesley. I see, Miss Shepherd. No, that's perfectly all right. Just give me five minutes, then show them in."

He replaced the receiver, his shocked nerve centers clamoring for relief. He glanced automatically at the Field Sports Calendar on the mantel. The date of Annesley's release from jail was ringed with black crayon — 27 June. Ariane had disappeared the night of the 26th.

He opened the drawer by his knee. The buff envelope with the keys to the Kinnerton Street apartment was still there. It had been returned by a cabdriver on Saturday morning — no covering note, no explanation. He had canceled an appointment and rushed around to Kinnerton Street, opened the door with hopeless disbelief. Everything he had given Annesley's wife over the months had been set out on the hall table. A few unopened bottles of scent, some pieces of costume jewelry, a leather handbag still in its original wrappings. The furnished flat had been completely cleared of the rest of her belongings.

He closed the drawer and went to the window. The air outside was pungent with the smell of low tide. Gulls wheeled high in the sunshine. The railed-off patch of grass made a buffer between the calm of King's Bench Walk and the diesel-growl of the Embankment.

He wiped his hands on his handkerchief, looking round the room. Half-paneled walls lifted to an original Adams ceiling. The volumes of case law and pink-tied briefs belonged to another generation. Two tall bookcases enclosed them. He crossed the room, watching the reflection in the mirror advance to meet him. It was gray-haired with solid shoulders well tailored in blue hopsack. The face wore the confident smile of the courtroom.

He turned away, seeing himself as he'd be standing in front of the Disciplinary Committee of the Law Society — middle-aged and vulnerable. The charge would be unanswerable. "Conduct unbecoming a solicitor." He had far too much at stake to let things go that far. The collapse of his law practice would be only part of the disaster. The whole underpinning of bluff and pretense that supported his credit would disintegrate overnight.

He straightened his back as the door opened. Annesley and his wife were strangely alike in appearance. They had the same pale hair and arrogant noses. Only the eyes were completely different. The girl's bulged slightly — with gray, smoky pupils. Annesley's were the color of cracked flint, and restless. He was wearing a chalk-striped flannel suit and drab suede boots. The girl's blue linen dress was sleeveless. She moved her bare legs in the hesitant saunter of a model making an entrance. Annesley held her elbow, tall and solicitous. He waited till the door closed on Venner's secretary, pulled a chair for his wife and perched on the armrest.

"You'd better make sure we won't be disturbed. I don't think you'd want anyone else to hear what I'm going to say, Venner."

Venner put the desk between them. He propped his elbows, studying the younger man's expression thoughtfully.

"I already have," he said quietly.

Annesley's hand dropped down on his wife's shoulder. She leaned idly into the pressure of his palm, smiling up at him. He shifted the caress to the nape of her neck. His voice was easy.

"Good. Then you know why I'm here?"

The ruler turned endlessly in Venner's fingers. The combination of the girl's lies and his own wishful thinking had always made the possibility seem remote. He hedged.

"Not until you tell me, no."

Annesley's eyes opened very wide. "Come off it! Ariane has been completely frank. She was lonely and you took advantage of the situation. You ought to be ashamed of yourself, old boy. A lawyer has no business having an affair with a client's wife."

Venner took a deep breath. The girl gave him look for look. Memory revived the darkened bedroom, her cheek beside his on the pillow. Her face had worn the same faint smile then — his interpretation of its meaning had been fatuous. He lifted a warning hand.

"You've had a rough time, Michael. I wouldn't want to see you land yourself in more trouble. You'd better listen to me. Your mother gave me a certain sum for legal expenses. Your appeal happened to cost less than we had anticipated. Mrs. Annesley came here for help and I applied the balance we held to your credit. I have her receipts, Michael, and that will be my story. Nothing more, nothing less."

Annesley uncrossed his legs and stood up. "I'm sure you have all the right pieces of paper. But it's not as simple as that. Ariane's a truthful girl. And she's quite ready to swear that she's been to bed with you on a number of occasions."

"Seventeen." She might have been remembering a series of parking offenses. "The first time at Rowland Gardens, the rest at Kinnerton Street."

Annesley's shoulder lifted. "You see. If she has to, she'll admit that to the Law Society. It'll be an unpleasant experience for her, of course, but she'll do it."

Venner's hand hovered above the office phone. "I think we'll have witnesses to the rest of this conversation," he said evenly.

A couple of days at liberty had put a glow on Annesley's jail pallor.

"By all means," he said. "If that's what you really want. But I do think you should hear the rest of it first." He paused with an actor's sense of timing.

Venner's fingers crept back to his lap. Ariane had

played to his conceit perfectly. Always grateful and promising more than she gave — a little bewildered by the future. They had spent a great deal of time considering the best way of divorcing Annesley. He smiled thinly.

"You're forgetting the weakness of your own position, Michael. It wouldn't be the first time this sort of thing's been tried on. A chap comes out of prison with a grudge against his lawyer, so he makes this sort of accusation. There are ways of dealing with it, of course. I'd rather not use them — if only for your mother's sake."

Annesley teetered, his heels hooked over the brass fender. He dragged his eyebrows together.

"What a lot of balls you talk, Venner. 'For your mother's sake!' The respectable solicitor with a bleeding heart and hot little hands. Remember what you said to me before we went into court — what can't be proven doesn't exist in law. I never forgot it. Take a look at these!" He reached inside his jacket pocket and skidded an envelope across the desk.

Venner lifted the ungummed flap. The envelope contained a dozen reproductions of thumb and fingerprints. One reproduced an entire hand. A dated signature was scrawled across the bottom of each card. Annesley swept the prints back in their envelope, his manner dry.

"I thought you'd be impressed by the Belton Detective Agency. If a retired Scotland Yard officer's word isn't above suspicion, where the hell would we be? Belton lifted these prints yesterday round at Kinnerton Street. They were all over the place — in the kitchen, the lavatory and the bedroom. The palm print came from the side of the bed. He's willing to testify as an expert that these prints all belong to the same person. *I'm* the one who'll say that they're yours."

Venner lifted his eyes from his fingers. The younger man's eyes were as hard as the flint they resembled. He wet his lips cautiously. The office had used the Belton Detective Agency a dozen times in the past. His mind leapt inventively. He could give the principal a tale of an unnamed client who was being subjected to black-mail. If the ex-cop had the negatives there was still a chance. He made his voice and expression reasonable.

"I think we're both sensible enough not to do any-thing hasty, Michael. I mean something we'd be sorry for afterwards. I'm admitting nothing — but this isn't the time or place to reach a conclusion. As soon as I've finished here, I'll meet you anywhere you like and talk this thing over."

The girl's throat swelled. A swatch of pale hair swung across her eyes. She laughed.

"For tea! He might even bring his wife, Michael. This scheming bitch with a cash-register instead of a heart. It's *terrible!* Do you realize something — as long as poor Stephen keeps earning the money she doesn't care *where* he spends his nights!"

Annesley's curtness stopped her dead. He turned on Venner, his face hostile.

"You lie about as easily as you breathe, Venner. But you've used the oratory on me once too often. I was a mug not to realize why you wanted me to plead guilty. I had to go inside to learn why. In fact, I learned *all* about Venner and Venner. The big show they put up for

the hard-core pros while people like me get thrown to
the lions. Jail gave me time to think. And I used it."

Venner did his best with an assumption of defiance.

"You don't really suppose I'll stand for blackmail, do
you, Michael? How could I — a man in my position?"

Annesley's lips grew thin. "You will, old boy. You've
overreached yourself this time. *I've* got the negatives
of those fingerprints. Not only that, I've had Belton's
statement notarized. Tell me something — did you ever
hear of anyone called Herbert Connolly?"

Venner tried the name over in his mind without echo.
"No," he said cautiously.

Annesley settled his jacket. "You will. He's a milkman on the early round. He reached Kinnerton Street
just after seven in the morning. He remembers a man
coming out of 120 on the 23rd of June. The chap bought
a half-pint of milk from the trolley and drank it there.
Fortyish, the milkman said. Well-dressed. 'Dead respectable, guv'nor — like one of these City blokes.' "

The imitation was well done. It seemed to reach Venner's thudding eardrums from a great distance.

"What exactly is it you want, Michael?" he asked.

Annesley took a few steps, head hanging, hands deep
in his trouser pockets.

"Five thousand pounds!" he said suddenly.

Venner blinked. "Five thousand . . . you're both
out of your minds. You can't get away with a thing like
this."

Annesley's eyes were ringed like a bird's and unwink-
ing.

"Why can't I? Because prisons are filled with people

who've tried and made a mess of it? I said I didn't waste my time, Venner. You ought to know how lawbreakers like to talk about their exploits. I listened to anyone who had anything to say about blackmail. The park queers, the real pros with files. They all had the same story, basically. A blackmailer has two things to worry about. The anonymity the cops offer to the heroes who'll prosecute; and killing the laying goose. Neither of these things worries me. Do you know why?"

Venner ran a finger round the inside of his collar. Mr. X was no refuge. There wasn't an assize court in the country where this ruse would protect him if he prosecuted. There'd always be acquaintances at the solicitors' bench who'd know the real identity of Mr. X. Barristers — possibly the judge himself. And when it was all over, they'd bring Annesley from jail. He would still have to face the pair of them in front of the Disciplinary Committee. Before he started to fight, he had a perverse wish to hear the worst from Annesley.

"Suppose I tell you to go to hell?" he asked steadily.

Annesley's expression changed. He leaned across the desk so that the slightest nuance of his message would register.

"Then I'll ruin you. Your name'll stink so high you won't even be able to get a job serving writs."

Venner lit a cigarette, releasing the smoke in a long dribble. Odd that the decision was being forced on him. In a way he was glad. The old recurring dream was coming close to reality — to walk softly away into a completely new existence, oblivious to everything left behind. His plan was as old as the dream and dangerous.

But at least it was better than scandal and bankruptcy. The first thing to do was to keep this pair thinking of him as a cowed dog jumping through the hoops they held.

He coughed on the end of a nervous laugh. "And it doesn't occur to you that I might not *have* five thousand pounds?"

The girl's swift accusation came venomously.

"No, it doesn't. You never stopped bragging about the money you had to make to satisfy your wife's extravagance — the jewelry you'd bought her. And came crawling round to me with a twenty-five shilling bottle of scent."

Venner looked squarely at her husband.

"This practice has been going downhill for the last six years, Michael. No matter what you've heard or think, that's a fact. I wouldn't even be able to pay my staff if it weren't for my wife. Her money bought the house we live in — the car I drive — her jewelry. *Everything!*"

"He's lying, Michael," the girl insisted. "I know it."

Annesley silenced her. "I'll tell you what I think, Venner. That you've got all the instincts of a snake and none of its courage. The point is that I don't care *whose* money it is — as long as you get it!"

Venner's fingers made a canopy under which he stared morosely.

"Just like that, eh? I go to my wife and ask her for five thousand pounds and get it. You don't know what you're talking about. I'd need a reason as valid as eating."

"You've got one," Annesley said curtly.

Venner took his hands from his forehead.

"You mean you'll really push me that far?"

"I'll dance on your grave," answered Annesley.

Venner was quiet for a moment. "No, I'm a lawyer," he said at last. "I've seen too much of this. Once you get the taste you'll be back for more, Michael."

Annesley's hand rapped the desk for emphasis. "Listen, anyone who robs the same bank twice is a fool. Not only that, you're cunning enough to work out some sort of answer as time goes on. Before that happens we'll be in Australia."

Venner's tone was frank. "Time's exactly what I need if I'm going to produce this money."

Annesley turned from the bookcase. The faint sneer on his mouth seemed permanent.

"Oh really? What lousy little trick's lurking at the back of your mind — having me picked up on some phony charge? You always did brag about the people you knew at the Yard. You'd better remember this — I'll shout as loud inside as I would out."

Venner shook his head. "I'm not that sort of fool. I repeat, I need time."

Annesley relinquished the words reluctantly.

"How much?"

Venner shrugged with the right degree of uncertainty.

"How can I answer that, Michael? A month — two. I'll have to try to find a story that will convince my wife — put it to her in the proper climate of thought. It might even be necessary to take her away for a bit."

The girl was swinging a bare leg, her mouth sardonic.

"Touching — a sort of second honeymoon! If you listen to a word he's saying, Michael, you're insane."

Annesley covered her lips with his hand. "Ssh — you're talking too much. It's a pity that your important clients can't see you now, Venner. I used to lie awake in that stinking cell at night wondering when you were going to catch on. It didn't seem possible that a grown man *wouldn't* — even if he *was* hooked below the navel. You're old, Father William. And you're not even smart. I'll give you a month."

Venner's raised eyes held the shaky challenge of a bad poker player bluffing a weak hand.

"Without either of you coming here or to the house? I've got to have that much security, Michael. You can push a desperate man to the same extremes as a brave one!"

The girl spoke acidly from behind her makeup mirror.

"You're neither. You're nothing but a big whine with varicose veins."

He was glad his hands were under the desk. He dug his nails deep in his palms. Annesley grinned cheerfully.

"The talent for saying the right thing at the wrong time. But I imagine you're familiar with it by now. Don't worry. Neither of us will come near you. Where would you take your wife?"

"I don't know," Venner said promptly. "Any more than I know what I'll say to her. Quite possibly nowhere. It depends on circumstances."

Annesley loped over to the fireplace. He picked up

the calendar, smiling as he saw his release date ringed with crayon. He flipped the pages to the following month.

"Let's say the first of August," he said easily. "I'll be here at ten o'clock sharp. Don't worry about cash. I'll take a check. I've drawn up a contract. I get five thousand pounds for a valuable consideration."

Venner slumped, allowing himself the beginnings of a smile. Amateurs handling high explosives. All he had to do was wait till they blew themselves skyhigh.

"A contract, Michael. What good can that do?"

Annesley spoke over his shoulder. "None, maybe. It just makes me feel better. You see, I've written this outline of a story that I think has possibilities. It's about a young actor who goes to jail. While he's inside, his wife is unfaithful with the lawyer who defends him. The story's the valuable consideration."

The girl burst into renewed laughter, wiping her eyes with a handkerchief.

"I'm sorry, darling, I can't help it. It's his expression. He looks exactly the same as he did when the magistrate sentenced you. As though someone just snatched his meal from in front of him."

Venner scraped his chair back. "I think you'd better go. The walls aren't that thick. All right — the first of August, Michael. I wish I had as much faith in your side of the bargain."

Annesley collected his wife's elbow with gallantry.

"I've heard that people pray for faith. You ought to try it. Don't get up. We'll see ourselves out."

The girl said goodbye, her face still mocking. Venner

made no attempt to hide the sudden hatred he felt for her.

"If I thought you'd swing for it," he said suddenly, "I'd be happy to blow my brains out. I just wanted you to know that, Ariane."

Annesley opened the door. *"What* brains?" he asked deliberately and closed the door behind them.

Venner reached for the pile of outgoing mail. He heard Annesley's laugh through the open window. He started signing letters, keeping his head bent till their footsteps no longer sounded on the pavement. He took the office phone.

"Ask Mr. Sharp to come in, will you, Miss Shepherd? And tell him to bring the Diary with him."

The managing clerk was a spare, rusty-haired man clamped into an old-fashioned starched collar. The faint lines of fuzz that served him as eyebrows were bent in a look of permanent anxiety. He wore striped trousers and a black jacket and moved his legs quietly as though he were in court.

"You wanted me, Mr. Venner?"

Venner nodded. Nothing he said or did must seem out of the ordinary. Sharp's memory bordered on total recall.

"What's the position with regard to Santa Eulalia, Arthur? Can we still get it for a month or six weeks?"

Sharp's grin showed the stained teeth of a confirmed pipe smoker.

"You've already got it if you want it. The agents called last week when you were at the County of London Sessions. I could remember thinking at the time that you were impressed with the photographs they sent round. So I took an option. Does this mean that you've finally made up your mind about your summer holiday, sir?"

Venner smiled, linking the clerk in understanding. "Mrs. Venner made up our minds. She decided last night that what we both needed was a holiday in Spain. I don't know what she'll say at the end of it. Do you see my wife on an island without electricity, Arthur? With no maid and scorpions in the bathroom?"

Sharp worried the question to a cautious answer. "I don't know about that, sir. I'm thinking about Mrs. Sharp. Last year she chose Margate. We spent eleven days out of fourteen on the pier watching the rain come down. Restful, she said it was. I mean — if the idea's theirs to start with it seems to make a difference, doesn't it?"

"I think you're a philosopher, Arthur," said Venner. "What does the Diary look like?"

Sharp turned the pages, loyally refusing the significance of those left blank.

"It's easy, Mr. Venner — that's because they've got light calendars at the Sessions and Central Criminal Court. Fletcher's up at the Guildhall on the twelfth but that's routine. I thought of briefing George Fell. We hardly need anyone stronger at this stage. Fletcher will certainly be committed."

Venner explored his instep with the tip of the ruler. The first alarm of the Annesley's visit was wearing off. His mind was already putting the solution into practice.

"That seems perfect, Arthur. What it really means is that there's no reason why I shouldn't get away at the

end of the week. You'd better get onto the agents immediately — send them a month's rent. And while I think
of it, get Miss Shepherd to make out a check in favor of
the Paragon Insurance Company — a hundred and
eighteen pounds. Tell her to mark the stub 'premium.' "

Sharp glanced up from his penciled notes, his eyes
curious.

"That's a new policy, isn't it — Paragon Insurance?"

"It goes with the holiday, Arthur," Venner answered
lightly. "It's one of these short-term comprehensive
deals. They cover one against loss of baggage, cash —
your medical expenses and all that sort of thing. And
there's a personal accident clause. I suppose I must be
worth *something* to the firm. Everyone seems to be doing
it and the premium is deductible."

Sharp's voice was mildly envious. "It's funny the way
a chap hankers after an island, isn't it, Mr. Venner? It's
always been a dream of mine. Sitting in a boat somewhere in the sunshine with a rod. It'd almost be like
sliding into someone else's skin. No worries at all —
that's if you went alone, of course."

Venner sneaked a quick look. The other man's expression was innocent.

"Your back blisters and you get dysentery," Venner
said shortly. "And you never *are* alone. I'm going home
early, Arthur. The letters are signed. Don't forget the
checks."

Sharp shook his head. "I won't. Do I take it you won't
be in for the rest of the week, sir—just so that I know
what to say?"

Venner stood up. "In and out. If anything really important comes up, you can always reach me at home or leave a message."

Alone in the afternoon sunlight, he followed the aimless buzzing of a bluetailed fly. Everyone imagined he knew Stephen Venner. The Annesleys — Sharp — Purcell at the bank. And of course, Emma. Emma more than anyone. Yet none of their assessments was accurate. He'd assembled the components of his master plan under their very noses — to be used in the nick of time like the hero in an old-fashioned melodrama. Now Emma had to be made part of it.

He walked over to the window and swatted the fly viciously. Emma would move fast enough once she realized that the alternative to his scheme was disaster. He unlocked the cupboard at the end of the bookcase. His police permit was five years old but the weapon still wore its original film of grease. He wrapped the .32 automatic in paper and dropped it in his briefcase. He dug deeper into the cupboard and carried the papers he found to the desk. He spread the blue proposal form in front of him and studied the operative clause.

Section 2 PERSONAL ACCIDENT (rate ten shillings per thousand pounds.)

a. death or loss of one or more limbs and/or one or both eyes.
b. permanent disablement other than loss of limbs and/ or eyes.
c. temporary disablement (benefit payable for 104 weeks.)

d. temporary partial disablement (benefit payable for 104 weeks.)

He completed the form carefully.

1. Proposer's name in full: Stephen Digby Venner
2. Address: Heronscourt, Kingston Hill, Kingston, Surrey.
3. Occupation: Solicitor.
4. Age: Forty-three.
5. Names of persons traveling with proposer: Emma Jane Venner.
6. Period of holiday: 5 July, 1964, to 5 August, 1964.
7. Details of journey: By plane and train to Los Gatos, Province of Huelva, Spain.

I hereby declare that I and the members of my party are in good health and free from physical defect or infirmity and I know of no good reason why the company should not grant this insurance and I agree to accept the company's policy.

Signed: STEPHEN DIGBY VENNER

He buzzed his secretary. "I'm just off, Miss Shepherd. Will you bring in that check for the Paragon people?"

He sealed the check and proposal form in an office envelope. If he mailed it on his way home, the company's letter of acceptance ought to be in his possession within the next forty-eight hours. A man of his standing would never be refused. The Law List still counted for something. He took his hat and briefcase and left the building by the door that gave directly on to the hallway. Steps outside led to a narrow street that twisted away northward. Open doors gapped the fronts of the houses, offering glimpses of hand-carved banisters and uncarpeted stairs. Painted boards and brass plates bore the names of barristers and solicitors occupying chambers within. He lifted a hand at a middle-aged man wearing a wig and gown. He must remember to be generous with the cheerful, jaunty smile. Every contact he had now could well be an excuse for some bore's recollections later.

He dropped the letter to the insurance company into the mail slot with a sense of finality. Every decision he made from here on would be linked to another still more dangerous. And it would go on like that till society finally accepted his staged exit. The prospect was oddly exciting.

Forty minutes later, he swung the Mercedes up Kingston Hill. Another quarter mile and he turned off onto a graveled driveway. Red brick walls enclosed a couple of acres of trees and grass. Mauve-splashed creeper covered the long house, rambling round white-painted windows. A bright, polished interior was visible through the open front door. He drove through a gate in the privet hedge screening the garage. The married couple who ran Heronscourt lived in the flat above. He edged the Mercedes in beside his wife's small convertible. He felt the radiator of Emma's car — it was cold. He entered the house, through a hall hung with hunting prints. Every door was wide to the breeze. Raw-silk summer curtains rustled in the drawing room. He locked his briefcase in the library safe and stood in the corridor listening. The kitchen radio was on. There was no sign of Emma.

At the head of the stairs were two self-contained apartments. He opened his own door. It had been a long time since either Emma or he had gone into one another's rooms uninvited. He kicked his clothes in a heap on the dressing-room floor and walked into the bath naked. He braced himself, blowing as the cold needles of water hit his back. He wrapped himself in a thick towel and went to the bedroom window. His wife was lying on the terrace directly underneath. She was on her back, her face and head covered with a chiffon scarf. He looked down at her dispassionately. At thirty-seven, she was still able to wear a bikini with grace. The planes and angles of her body offered a completely misleading promise of voluptuousness. He put on slacks and a tennis shirt and pushed his bare feet into moccasins. The gilt and ormolu clock in the drawing room showed ten minutes past six. He poured himself an outsize martini and padded out to the terrace. Emma started violently at the sound of his voice. She rolled over, scattering the creams and suntan lotion at her side. Her muscles unsheathed like an animal's as she stretched. She lifted herself on an elbow, the scarf dropping round her wide, tanned shoulders. Straight beech-colored hair plunged to her neck, the last few inches turning back on themselves. She wore no lipstick and looked at him out of hostile, jade eyes.

"One of these days you'll start moving round the house like a normal human being instead of one of your burglar clients."

He rolled the dryness of the gin on his tongue, wondering exactly how she construed a "normal human being."

"Are the Collinses in or out?" he asked.

She shrugged. "How should I know? I imagine she's in the annex — and I heard him cutting grass. Is it important?"

He balanced his glass on the edge of the cane chair. A dozen sycamore trees lined the far side of the lawn, their summer foliage hiding the ugliness of television aerials beyond.

"You don't know it, Emma, but today's a milestone in your life. For the last seventeen years you've managed to live extremely uselessly at my expense. All of a sudden, unless you start using your head, that's going to come to a complete standstill."

She swung good brown legs from the mattress, testing the warmth of the red tiles with painted toes. She gave him a long hard stare.

"Tell me something, Stephen — is she presentable or does she need a bath like the rest of them?" The look of assessment hardened into a familiar mask of disgust.

He shrugged. "Does that sort of remark make you feel superior, or what is it exactly?"

Her fingers curled round her lighter. The cigarette between her lips bobbed as she spoke.

"For a lawyer, you're remarkably unsubtle, Stephen. Don't you think I know all the signs by now? Every time you find some little tramp with a blond rinse who'll listen to the sad story of your life, you turn up here with the same look on your face. You're wasting your time —

I have absolutely no intention of giving you a divorce — ever."

He ran his thumb and forefinger slowly down the crease in his trouser leg.

"You made that plain a long time ago. I want you to listen to this carefully. A few months ago I defended a man who went to prison. While he was inside, I had an affair with his wife. They both came into the office this afternoon, demanding five thousand pounds. If I don't pay, they threaten to go to the Law Society. There's no question whether they prove their case, they could do it four ways."

She came bolt upright on the mattress, her narrowed eyes veiled by cigarette smoke.

"I don't believe you," she decided. "Even you wouldn't be that big a fool."

He spoke sarcastically. "That sounds odd coming from you. I thought that as far as you were concerned there was no limit to my stupidity. They want five thousand pounds by the first of August — *dear*."

She shook herself as though the threat were something tangible she could dislodge.

"Five thousand pounds. Don't be ridiculous. It doesn't make sense."

"It makes more sense than an appearance in front of the Disciplinary Committee," he said tartly. "Have you any idea what I'm worth, Emma?"

She looked at him blankly. "None at all. You've never encouraged me to ask."

He turned his hands over, staring into the cradle they made.

"I'm four years behind on my income-tax payments. The bank has had the deeds to King's Bench Walk since last November. I have exactly four hundred and thirty-seven pounds in my account and no hope of an extended overdraft. There's nothing left to extend it *on*."

Her eyes shaded to the color of rockbound water. "What about the police?"

His mouth mocked her. "What about them? Why don't you come with me to Scotland Yard — tell them what a decent fellow I really am, Emma?"

She looked away. "It wouldn't have been difficult to have found what you wanted, surely. London is full of lonely women. But naturally you had to choose the wife of a client. Have you ever once stopped to consider me in whatever you do, Stephen — just once? But now I'm expected to hold your hand and defend you."

"You're expected to defend yourself," he corrected. "Or don't you want to keep all this?" He waved at the stock-scented garden, warm and peaceful in the evening sun.

She took a deep breath. "I'll keep it, Stephen," she said uncompromisingly. "You can be sure of that — I'll keep it."

He linked hands behind his neck. "Not unless you're prepared to do some pretty drastic fighting for it, you won't. If the Annesleys ever get as far as the Law Society we're sunk — ruined. I'll tell you what'll happen the day after I come in front of the Disciplinary Committee, shall I — the bailiffs will move in here. Once I'm struck off the List, they'll be falling over themselves to make me bankrupt, the Internal Revenue people heading the charge. There's one way of blocking disaster but I need your help for it."

Her look was sly. "Any time you need my help I'm suspicious, Stephen. I'm by no means as stupid as you seem to think I am. For instance, I wouldn't dream of selling a single piece of jewelry to give to these people. It would be pointless anyway. They'd only be back for more, blackmailers always are."

He scotched the idea hurriedly. "That wasn't what I had in mind. This is something much more drastic. I've seen the end of the road for some time. Annesley's an incidental. I don't intend to give him a penny."

She lifted curious eyes. "Then what?"

He went inside and fixed a couple of drinks. She took hers, still very intent on his expression. He spoke with weight and emphasis.

"Whether or not you like it, it's as much your future at stake now as mine, Emma. Just how far would you be willing to go to protect it?"

"How far am I meant to go?" she asked quietly.

He set his glass down. "Murder. For a half share in a hundred thousand pounds."

She arched her back, slitting her eyes against the sun. "You're joking of course."

He shook his head. "Remember the island — the one off the coast near Huelva — I took it for a month this afternoon. At the same time, I insured myself for a hundred thousand pounds. Does that sound like a joke to you?"

She touched her throat nervously. "You insured what — your life? I don't follow the sense of all this — you're hardly the suicidal type."

The breeze was cool in his damp hair. "I'm not going to die. Somebody else will do that in my place. Somebody roughly my height and build. That's where you come in. He'll be found with my passport — all you have to do is identify the body as your husband's."

Some of her drink slopped on the terrace. She hunched, watching the ants investigate its sweet stickiness. It was some time before she replied.

"I'd rather you told me this is a joke, Stephen."

He lolled back in the chair. "Fifty thousand pounds. For identifying a stranger's body as mine. That's all you're being asked to do."

She spoke much more quietly. "You keep talking about a stranger — as though you could walk into a self-service store and find what you want."

He eased into practiced persuasiveness. Once she committed herself, she would fight without giving or asking quarter.

"I've got a week to look. He'll be the sort of chap who can leave a bed-sitter in the slums and never be heard of again. Someone without friends or relatives to worry about his disappearance — a failure. And the place to find failures is in a police court. That's where I'm going to start looking tomorrow."

The sun dipped below the boundary wall. She shivered and dragged the cashmere sweater over her head. She shook out her hair. The copper cascade fell straight and divided about her face.

"I don't think I like the idea of being an accessory to murder, Stephen," she said obstinately.

His manner hardened. "Since when did the sanctity of any life but your own matter to you? You're being offered fifty thousand pounds on a plate. What are you frightened of?"

She dragged the sweater below her knees. "You. All your faults are those of a weak man — that's what I'm afraid of."

He wiped the soreness from the corners of his eyes. The time had come for blunter instruments.

"There's something that might help to make up your mind, Emma. Heronscourt is in my name, remember. I've no intention of hanging on here till they come banging on the front door. If your answer's no, I'll raise what I can on this place and leave the country. But I'll leave alone. You've got until tomorrow morning to think it over."

Her pupils shaded darker. "That sounds much more in character. Am I allowed to ask why it should be so easy to defraud an insurance company of a hundred thousand pounds?"

His answer was swift. "Because they're insuring a life and I propose to give them a dead body. That's the basic reason."

Her fingers were working steadily, massaging the skin over her temple.

"Just imagine — you must have been sitting there all this time with this scheme in your head and saying nothing. What if there hadn't been any blackmail — I suppose you'd have vanished one day with everything you could lay your hands on and left me biting my thumbs?"

The thrust was too near the truth to be treated lightly. "That's the obvious interpretation for you to make. The stark truth is that we need one another to survive. The plan requires at least a temporary alliance and we're the beneficiaries of the plan. Try to look at it like that."

She reached automatically for her pack of cigarettes. "If I were to be an accomplice in what you call survival, I'd have to be very sure of my fifty thousand pounds, Stephen."

"You would be," he pointed out. "I've spent a great deal of time safeguarding our interests. The way I've worked it, neither of us can be tempted to run out on the other. Your position as my widow is unassailable. My will is with the bank — if you use them for probate it will simplify matters. We'll have to come to an arrangement about death duties. There'll be a fifty percent charge on the estate in favor of Horus A.G. The rest is yours."

She shifted her legs. "And who is Horus A.G.?"

"Me," he said simply. "A Swiss company, just two signatures away."

She came out of some secret and involved calculation. "I'll give you this, Stephen — you've always had the touch for convincing detail. Just how do you propose to get your victim to Spain?"

He poured the rest of his drink over the ants. "I'll answer that once I've found him. However it's done, I'd obviously need your help."

She answered almost absentmindedly. "I can see that.

I suppose I'd better tell Mrs. Collins you're in for dinner. You weren't expected." Her smile was malicious.

He rubbed the spot between his eyebrows. "One way or another I want to know by the morning — is that understood?"

She turned in the doorway. "It's understood. After seventeen years in the wilderness, I'm suddenly madly important. That's life, isn't it, Stephen?"

Ross MacLaren — Tuesday 30 June 1964

H<small>E WAS</small> sitting with his back against the wall. The lower half of his body was thrust squarely across the sidewalk. The early morning gusts had deposited dust, discarded bus tickets and a torn paper sack under his left trouser leg. A neon sign over his head flashed on and off at regular intervals, reflected in the store window on the other side of the street.

With each click of the time switch MacLaren's eyes opened on the headless models opposite. Their legs were finely tapered and they had improbable breasts packed into brief bras. There was a chalked message on the easel in the window: BE BOLD THIS SUMMER! WEAR SUMMIT-LIFT!

Hearing the approaching footsteps, he forced a show of dignity into his expression. A pair of black boots came into focus. He lifted his eyes, taking in the police uniform, the young face under the helmet. He grinned, pleased that the thought came swiftly and clearly.

"Twelve o'clock and all's well, officer."

The cop straddled, hitching a thumb under the flap of his breast pocket.

"You can't sleep here, you know. Come on, you'll have to get up. On your feet."

MacLaren's smile held. In the cop's left-hand pocket would be a notebook. H.M. Stationery Office issue. And a little pencil with a blunt point. He raised himself on an elbow.

"Nobody can do without the pause that refreshes, constable. We all need it. It's necessary for the next day's labor."

A truck's air brakes hissed as it halted for the signals. The first glow of dawn touched the adjacent square, bringing color and texture to the Victorian masonry. A blackbird called from the top of a plane tree. The cop was obviously unimpressed with it all.

"You want to play the fool, mate, and you'll get all the rest you need — in the nick."

MacLaren rolled away from the outstretched hand to lie pensively on his side. The scale of social values had to be rearranged. This "mate" business was a danger signal.

"I'll take care of the street for you," he said loudly. ". . . the most outstanding recruit to crime-reporting in years — known for his tact and integrity. It'll all be here in the morning, *mate*."

The cop pushed back his helmet. "I didn't know they made it that strong. You stink like a distillery. I'll give you ten seconds to make up your mind — which'll it be — home or the nick?"

"Cossack!" retorted MacLaren. "Your whip's showing. A drunk is a drunk is a drunk. And if you haven't been exposed to a poetical education that's Blessed Mother Repetitia. You want me, carry me!"

He slid down till his shoulder blades touched the sidewalk. He felt the near-empty bottle in his hip pocket smash. He lay spread-eagled, his mind growing cunning as he heard the cop's easy tread to the police box — the one-sided telephone conversation. It was only minutes till the low-geared snarl of the police tender invaded the empty street. Somebody dragged him upright. He collapsed contentedly into a frogmarch that took him to the waiting wagon. He pitched forward into a darkness smelling of carbolic and groped for the seat.

Round Two coming up, with the first even. This one depended on whether or not he could guess the charge they'd hit him with. The permutations were limited but his hunch was usually wrong. Drunk and incapable; Drunk and disorderly; Drunk and on enclosed premises. He settled for the first and tried to orient himself. He'd been drinking in Kensington. He must have been picked up somewhere in the neighborhood. That meant he'd be up at West London Police Court — tomorrow morning. Hell, no. This morning. He fumbled at an inside pocket, panic-stricken. Undoing the safety pin, he pulled out the two pound notes. He held them close to his mouth for a moment then stuffed them inside his left sock. He was still batting a hundred percent — they hadn't yet bagged him without his fine money on him. The wagon stopped. He stumbled towards the opening doors.

He climbed the four steps from the police-station yard, putting one foot in front of the other very deliberately. Once in the charge room, the two cops released their grips simultaneously. MacLaren's butt hit the bench with a jar that dislodged his bridgework. He nodded philosophically as he recognized the familiar furnishings. Ominous notices on the walls were illuminated by naked 100-watt lamps. A round-faced clock ticked away on top of a steel filing cabinet. Scrawled across a giveaway calendar was the thought "Whatever you do, you're wrong!"

His gaze settled on the heavy drooping shoulders and red melon head of the man inspecting him.

"Good evening," he said courteously.

The desk sergeant's voice was resigned. He made no secret of his apprehension.

"Gawd Almighty — if that isn't my bleeding luck! Two o'clock in the morning and see who I get for a customer. All right, officer, where'd you find him?"

MacLaren just failed to cross his legs. The young cop cleared his throat self-consciously.

"Flat on his arse outside Vogle's Delicatessen — that's Church Street, sarge. He asked for it. I gave him a chance to go on home."

The sergeant answered morosely. "A chance to go on home when he could come here and ruin my blood pressure! Not bloody likely."

Bile flooded MacLaren's throat — sweat broke out on his forehead. Leaning forward, he vomited violently on the floor.

"Get the mop," the sergeant said hopelessly. "And a bucket."

MacLaren staggered along the corridor as far as the

washroom. He kicked a pail under the faucet, peering miserably into the glass. His face was rough with stubble, his gray springy hair wild above black eyebrows. He carried the mop and pail back. The two men were silent as he cleared the mess.

"Sign the charge sheet," said the sergeant wearily, "and get back on your beat."

When the cop had gone, he bawled along the corridor. A red-faced jailer peered round the door leading to the cells.

"We've got Mr. MacLaren back to stay," said the sergeant. "Get his room ready." His face took on an expression of guile. "You'll feel better once you're lying down, Mac. How about getting the penwork over?"

MacLaren heard the charge with dull satisfaction. "Drunk and incapable." For once he'd hit it on the nose. He emptied his pockets on the desk, making a pile of matches, cigarettes, a few coins and a comb.

"The sergeant flicked a tear of ink from his pen. "They ought to open your head and see what you use for brains. Why is it we don't see you for a couple of years and then two or three nights on the trot. What *makes* a man like you a drunk?"

"Watch your language," MacLaren said severely. "I'm kicking the habit."

The sergeant turned his mouth down. "That'll be the day. How old are you, forty-two, isn't it?"

MacLaren started picking broken glass from his hip pocket, mutinously silent.

The sergeant's voice was cajoling. "I'll tell you what,

Mac. You help me and I'll see you get a nice hot cup of tea. How's that sound?"

"Like you've been drinking," said MacLaren.

The officer's face grew red. "I've got other things to do besides play around with you," he shouted. "What's your occupation?"

MacLaren put his possessions back in his pockets. "Wine-taster. That ought to give Sutcliffe a laugh."

The sergeant's expression brightened. "*Now* I've got some news for you. Your friend Sutcliffe's gone — retired. And the new bloke's mustard on drunks. Don't try any of your larks on him, I'm warning you."

MacLaren felt shock invade his body. Sutcliffe was part of an unchanging pattern, the five-minute appearance in front of the magistrate an exercise of the imagination. Sutcliffe's judgment of a drunk was moved entirely by the offender's flight of fancy. He had always accepted MacLaren's inventions as he used his nose-inhalant — noisily and with obvious satisfaction.

"A new guy," MacLaren said cautiously. "What's his name?"

The sergeant leaned his weight on his elbows. "Werner. He's a hero and a teetotaler, buster. Come on, let's have your occupation. I've got to put *something* on the sheet."

MacLaren buttoned his jacket very slowly. The line formed on the right, bridging the years. A dozen MacLarens, each a little more beat than his predecessor. Reporter — salesman — the dreary succession of jobs where the hired help kept ten percent of what they didn't make and tried to pay the rent with it. Occupation, the man said. How many ways were there of dignifying the word "bum"?

"Unemployed," he said in a loud voice. A drunk in the cells bawled encouragement.

"Where do you live?" said the sergeant.

MacLaren shrugged. That at least was no problem. No rent — no room, the guy had said three days ago.

"No fixed abode," he answered. The sergeant would like that — it had more style than "homeless."

The cop shut his book with relief. "It's half past two in the morning. I'm not going to start calling lawyers who never even heard of you, mate. I had enough of that the other night."

MacLaren started steering an erratic course towards the door to the cells. He spoke over his shoulder.

"Just inform the Commissioner of Police I'm here — he'd want to know."

The door was held open. The jailer's undershot jaw wagged like a cow chewing grass.

"Buggered if I know what you see in it."

MacLaren steadied himself against the wall. "That's because you live right."

The tongue of the lock shot home. He looked round the cell. The wooden bench had three palliasses stuffed with something resembling concrete chippings. One blanket that smelled of ten other people. A lavatory bowl—dripping under the barred window. The occupant of the next cell started to beat on the wall. MacLaren sat on the bench, took his shoes and tie off and stretched out. There were four hours' sleep ahead, then a scrape at the sink with last week's razor blade. A mug of sugar-less tea before the ride to court. The Black Maria would make its early morning round, the collector of human garbage. The labored image was his own — written long ago for the straphangers who read his column over some-one else's shoulder. A lousy piece of writing, maybe, but at least done with compassion.

He reached down for a shoe. Holding it by the toe, he clouted the wall hard a couple of times. The bang-ing from the next cell stopped immediately. He shut his eyes and fell into a troubled doze.

— The clock on the wall showed five minutes past ten. The door to the courtroom was ajar. The public gallery inside was already half full with regular spectators. Sneezing and coughing, they settled down for the morn-ing's entertainment. A woman in the front row was sob-bing into her husband's handkerchief. From time to time he patted her arm automatically, his eyes fixed on the dock.

MacLaren lit a cigarette with unsteady fingers. A few feet away, a couple of Flying Squad officers were joking with their prisoner. The three men wore the same con-fident grins under wary eyes, withdrawn in an in-timately closed society. MacLaren's escort blocked a yawn.

"A good job my old woman can't get her hands on you, chum. Do you realize I only went off duty at six o'clock? I've had one hour's kip — she gets up at seven to see the kids are ready for school. Do me a favor — get pissed on somebody else's manor next time."

MacLaren felt his hip gingerly. Glass splinters had
gone through his trousers, puncturing his right buttock.
It could have been worse, but then liquor treated him
kindly. He forgot but he rarely fell. He gaped in sympathy with the cop's yawn.

"I'll try to remember."

Movement began in the well of the court. The magistrate's clerk was rustling the papers on his desk. A bareheaded constable carried a carafe of water to the bench
with the tongue-balancing care of a choirboy. Mac-
Laren trod on his cigarette end. He had a brief glimpse
of a tall man, bent at the shoulders, sliding into the
magistrate's seat. Then the door was shut. His stomach
was already rumbling with apprehension. Courts had
affected him in the same way even as a reporter. Then
he had sat in the press box, the horns of his mind identifying with the prisoner in the dock. The feeling of op-
pression had lasted till the business of the day was over
and he left the building, using the exit like a human
being.

He crumpled the two pound notes in his moist palm.
The few shillings left would need careful investment. If
he had a bag he could check into some cheap hotel. But
to get his bag he needed the rent. It was no time to try
to work out that one. The door swung open. The jailer
called his name. MacLaren turned right into the dock,
standing as the clerk read from the charge sheet.

"You're charged with being drunk and incapable at
one-forty this morning at Church Street, Kensington. Do
you plead guilty or not guilty?"

MacLaren was aware of the magistrate's inspection. Werner was about his own age, dark and thin with an ascetic mouth. Like a militant parson, MacLaren decided. Cold showers to conquer the flesh and Divine Worship at the double. He shrugged.

"Drunk maybe but certainly not incapable. I was tired."

Someone tittered in the public gallery. The clerk's face reddened. He repeated the question in a loud, clear voice.

MacLaren spread his hands. "Not guilty then."

Werner drooped like a hawk preparing to swoop. "You may sit down."

The jailer plucked at MacLaren's sleeve. He sat facing the cop in the witness box. The man read from his notebook, using the stylized language of his calling.

". . . whereupon he rolled over, sir, and said 'carry me!' I summoned assistance and the defendant was removed to Church Street Police Station. His speech was slurred on arrival, sir, and he was unsteady on his feet."

Werner wrapped his forehead in both hands, his thin mouth working nervously.

"Did he offer any resistance to arrest, constable — I mean other than just sit there?"

The cop hesitated. He looked into his notebook as if the right answer were inscribed.

"Not what you'd call resistance, sir," he said finally. "He just sat there talking. Most of it nonsense."

Werner's mouth reshaped. "Have you any questions to ask the arresting officer, MacLaren?"

MacLaren had a feeling of intense rebellion. This guy was obviously going to fine him the limit. He might as well get his money's worth. He stood up, addressing the constable.

"What are your qualifications for judging the effect of alcohol on the human brain, officer?"

Werner's iciness cut through the ripple of amusement. "You needn't answer that question, constable. You may stand down. I find the charge proven." His face was thoughtful. "You give the impression that this is all very amusing for you, MacLaren. A rather boring sequel to the night's extravagance."

MacLaren shook his head. "I wouldn't call it boring, sir. Just inevitable. I have the fine on me."

"No doubt you have," the magistrate said blandly. He interrupted the jailer's account of MacLaren's previous arrests.

"How much do you know about this man, Mr. Wilbraham?"

The probation officer hauled himself up. Dandruff powdered his jacket collar. His eyes looked as if they had been born tired.

"Very little, I'm afraid, sir. I saw him twice about a year ago, then the day before yesterday. He refused offers of help on all three occasions."

It was difficult not to say something. Offers of help. A free ticket to Smarden Agricultural Colony where you dug potatoes under Guards discipline. Each inmate had the right to a thirty-second portion of a Nissen hut. There was piped music after labor as a concession to cultural needs.

He watched the magistrate's expression cautiously.

Werner probably prayed to a teetotal God for guid-
ance. The magistrate leaned forward.

"I'm going to remand you for sentence until tomorrow. I want to know something about this man, Mr. Wilbraham — whether or not anything can be done with
him."

MacLaren grabbed at the dock rail. "I said I had the
fine on me, sir."

Werner nodded. "Give the probation officer your
complete confidence, MacLaren. He's there to help you.
Next case."

The jailer twisted his fingers in MacLaren's sleeve. He
used his weight to hustle the Canadian out of court. Once
the steel pass door had slammed behind them, he released his grip and straightened his tunic.

"All yours, Fred. Twenty-four hours laydown."

The cells officer motioned MacLaren forward.

"Inside, dasher, and make yourself at home."

MacLaren sat down heavily. One of these days he'd
learn to act like a bum as well as look like one. He'd
clowned his way straight in here. All he'd had to do was
keep his big mouth shut — plead guilty and he'd have
been on the street with the rest of them. He broke one
of his five remaining cigarettes in two pieces, wondering where he'd spend the night — a remand prison or
back in the police station. Time was measured by the
court bailiff's bellow filtering through the walls. Once
the pass door opened on a couple of boy burglars, remanded for sentence like himself. Their shouts of mutual
congratulation revived his wonder at criminal optimism.

He soaked his handkerchief and started to clean his jacket. Suddenly a key was turned in the cell door. The probation officer's breezy manner was patently assumed for the occasion.

"I thought I'd nip in while court was adjourned," he said. "There are fewer people about."

MacLaren spread his damp jacket over the lavatory seat. The interview was obviously going to be under the Old Pals Act. "Let me be your friend" and the like. The sunlight that had conquered the grimed windows spread a griddle pattern on the wall. The pubs would be open on the North End Road. He pictured cool bars smelling of newly drawn beer, tilted bottles covering ice cubes with whisky. He wet his lips.

"Beat it!" he said briefly.

Wilbraham took a seat, steadying his knees with his hands. He had the peaked look of a dyspeptic. He dropped the bonhomie as if he too had never believed in it.

"You'd better revise your attitude, MacLaren. I've seen too many of your kind. Superior buggers it's a waste of time trying to help. But it is my job. And if you've got any sense, you won't make it more difficult than it already is."

MacLaren leaned against the patch of sunlight. "I said beat it — you and I have nothing to say to one another."

Wilbraham's mouth tightened. "How'd you like to be remanded for a week — not just a day? I can arrange that too, if that's what you want."

MacLaren pushed his hands firmly into his pockets.

Taking a swing at this character would be disastrous.

"All right," he said. "Let's trade. A bottle of beer for the sole rights to the story of my life."

Wilbraham's expression was patient. "Listen to me, MacLaren. Werner's new. He'll learn that chasing drunks is an unprofitable business. Especially your sort. But he's asked for a report and I'm going to give him one. It's up to you what sort of report. Use your head and you'll be out tomorrow."

MacLaren wiped the back of his neck. "There has to be something wrong with a system that treats sitting on an empty sidewalk as a crime."

"This is my lunch hour," Wilbraham broke in hurriedly. "I've got a weak stomach and I'm supposed to eat at regular intervals. Where you were born and things like that I can get from Records. Werner wants an object lesson in the evils of drink. If you can relate it to the truth, so much the better. Let's start with your employment history. Last time you were here, you described yourself as a crime reporter. Fact or fiction?"

MacLaren's self-appraisal was ironical. His clothes had been slept in for three nights running. And he needed a bath. Crime reporter! He took the cigarette Wilbraham offered.

"It's true enough. I started and finished on the *Globe*. Quote me if you like — 'a good man's hard to find in the business.'"

Wilbraham's pen jumped across the pad on his knees, his nose twitching like a rabbit's. He paraphrased MacLaren's information as he went.

". . . worked his way up to a position of responsibility . . . comfortable circumstances . . . What about your home life — are you married?"

Time honed the memory. The small apartment within sound of the animals in the zoo — the slammed front door the only escape from the hour-long arguments that moved from one room to another.

"Divorced."

Wilbraham nodded. "Then, I imagine, a period of maladjustment — terminating in a compulsive drinking habit. Isn't that it?"

MacLaren's cigarette smoke spiraled in the sunshine. This was like watching a silent film and adding your own captions. It was too easy for someone else to twist the sense of events. He reached across, taking the pad from Wilbraham's fingers. He tore off the two top sheets and flushed them down the lavatory.

"Not even for Werner," he said. "We'll tell it my way or not at all."

The color returned reluctantly to Wilbraham's cheeks. He shifted a shoulder in embarrassment.

"All right, let's do that."

MacLaren relaxed. This wasn't for anyone but himself. All he had to do was stay clear of words like honor and integrity. No one off the Voter's List had the right to use them.

"Go back to March, 1956. I was earning three thousand a year and expenses. There's no place on Fleet Street for a teetotaler. Stories break over a drink and as often as not you put them to bed that way. I can't remember ever being the worse for it. One morning a guy stuffed a wad of paper in his lock and walked out of the Appeal Court. He was doing fourteen years Preventive Detention and his name was Soldier Bailey."

Wilbraham broke open a roll of bismuth tablets.

"Another one of those victims of circumstance who break jail to prove their innocence. The police got him shortly afterwards if I remember correctly."

The hammering in MacLaren's chest came a little faster.

"They got him. I was working under an editor who coined the *Globe*'s motto, IN DEFENSE OF JUSTICE. Sands knew Bailey's escape had all the element of a good story. Drama and human interest. In this case, the mother — scrubbing floors to pay lawyers' fees. I had all the right contacts to find Bailey. I was able to walk into places where thieves congregate. Nobody pulled a razor on me — I was one of the regular guys. I got a story on its merits and never betrayed a confidence. Do you see the setup for Sands and the *Globe?*"

Wilbraham laid the pad on the floor by his feet, his eyes interested.

"I think so."

MacLaren went on talking as he paced the cell. "It took thirty-six hours to locate Bailey. I had to pledge my word to do it. Sands was offering five hundred pounds for the interview — and a promise to print Bailey's claims to innocence in full. Sands figured the piece would sell an extra hundred thousand copies. Only three people knew the time and place of the meeting. Bailey, Sands and me. Bailey had nothing to fear. We were meeting late at night near Hampton Court — it was winter. And he had my word. I was there first. I could hear him coming up the bank from the towpath. Suddenly cops started dropping out of the trees. There were six squad cars in the area and the *Globe*'s top photographer. They held Bailey there long enough for Sands to get a full spread of exclusive pictures. One shot showed Bailey with his eyes shut tight. A flashbulb must have exploded in his face. Nobody printed what he was bawling — but I heard it. It was meant for me personally. I've never forgotten. No money changed hands — Bailey's story never got into print."

Wilbraham's face was puzzled. "Didn't you expect your editor to inform the police? If he'd done anything else he'd have been compounding a felony."

MacLaren stopped dead. "Did you say you had a delicate stomach? Even Sands himself didn't dream up that one. Shut up and listen to the rest of it. It'll show you how naïve I was. I went over Sands' head to the Board with a charge of unethical conduct. I thought you could run a newspaper and still retain certain principles. I was out on my ear in two days. That was eight years ago. There hasn't been a newspaper in the country that would touch me ever since. Now go stuff that tender belly of yours and write your report. I want out of here."

Wilbraham hoisted himself up, wiping his mouth with the back of his hand.

"This is off the record. I've been at this job for twenty-six years. What's happened to you has happened to most of us, one way or another. Don't feel so sorry for yourself. I know as far as you're concerned I'm just another cop out of uniform — another eye to spit in. But I'd like you to believe this — if I knew how to help you I would."

MacLaren nodded. The guy probably meant it. "There's one thing I forgot," MacLaren said slowly. "The reason why I drink. It's because I think all honest endeavor has to be crowned with success. And I'll let you in on another secret. I don't even have to drink."

Wilbraham opened the cell door. "Catch hold of these. I'll see you in the morning." He pushed a couple of packs of cigarettes into MacLaren's hand and disappeared.

Stephen Venner — Thursday 2 July 1964

THE hall outside West London Police Court was still thronged with police and witnesses as Venner hurried out to the street. This was the sixth court he had covered in three days, varying his seat from the solicitors' bench to the public gallery. A vague indication of a watching brief had satisfied official curiosity about his presence. He made the occasional note, simulating an interest in the proceedings.

Half an hour ago, he had slipped into the back bench of the public gallery here. The first case on the day's list was called. He watched the tall, shabby figure into the dock with a sudden feeling of exultation. There was no need to look any further. *This was it.* The man's build, age and coloring were roughly his own. Each individual feature differed from his but there was a composite resemblance to his face that was striking. He listened to the banal charge, his trained mind seeing the obvious pattern of its disposal. He hurried outside.

The phone booth in front of the court building was

empty. He made three calls, obtaining the second number from the first, the last from the second. Then he hung up. In this sort of spot, having an acquaintance in the criminal aristocracy was of more use than knowing the Lord Chief Justice. His car was parked twenty yards away. He let the motor idle, looking back at the line of police vehicles. Two black Wolseleys stood fender to fender, their central aerials destroying any pretension to anonymity. The solitary Flying Squad car squatted openly in front of the courthouse. The driver was slumped on his shoulder blades, face lifted to the sun.

Venner pulled out. He kept an eye on the mirror till he was safe in the free-for-all of Hammersmith Broadway. After twenty years' association with the plain-clothes branch of the Metropolitan Police, he had a high regard for their ingenuity. The crew of a Flying Squad car had an interest in the public that was more catholic than the taxpayers suspected. Their inventiveness frequently matched that of their quarry. It ranged from the staked-out decoy car, unattended and laden with expensive-looking jewel cases, to the inspired shadowing of reputable criminal lawyers. Experience had taught him to beware the discreet tail as he drove to meet some vital witness designated to be a surprise. Neither side complained since the rules of the game were elastic.

He doubled back on his tracks and swung up the leafy rise of Campden Hill. A block short of Kensington High Street he stopped and walked the last quarter of a mile. A crescent-shaped street enclosed tall trees standing in unkempt grass. The bottom halves of some of the

Edwardian mansions had lapsed to commerce. There was a hat shop with a blazer-striped awning; a photographer's studio; a bow-windowed restaurant with tubbed hydrangeas and a menu exposed in longhand.

He slowed in front of a flight of steps leading down to a basement area. The iron railings had been painted gold. The sign over the door downstairs was in pica type lettering: william emerson rare books and prints.

He looked both ways up the street. A man with an apron was mopping the front of the restaurant. Two middle-aged matrons were talking their way into the hat shop. He ran down the steps, into the cool interior of the bookstore. Tweed-covered boards fitted into the window frames prevented passersby from looking down into the subterranean room. Artificial candles burned over the bookshelves. Stacks of unframed prints were scattered along a refectory table. His nose tracked the pungent smell to a joss stick smoldering in a piece of Dresden. He pulled a book at random from a shelf and started leafing through it. He turned slowly, conconscious that someone was watching him. A woman's head was thrust through the velvet curtain hanging against the back wall. Her flamboyant turban spiraled two feet into the air. Dead eyes regarded him from a stretched, unlined face. The skin appeared to have been lifted beyond further resiliency. She swayed through the curtains, advancing on ancient legs. Her short cotton dress fell off sluglike shoulders. She was wearing open-toe sandals. Her voice was theatrically deep.

"May I be of assistance to you, sir?"

"I wanted to see Mr. Emerson," he said casually.

Her old turtle eyes were suspicious. "Mr. Emerson is *never* here at this hour in the morning. If you'd care to leave your name . . ."

Venner put down his book. "He was here twenty minutes ago — I talked to him on the phone."

She picked up the book and dusted it thoroughly. She peered shortsightedly along the shelves until she found its slot. Her manner had grown a little more realistic.

"*What* did you say your name was?"

Her fingers fascinated him. They were extremely long and curved backwards from the second joint.

"Just say a friend of Mr. Coughlin's. You'll find that's all that's necessary."

She pulled the curtain back on its rail and vanished through a door in the wall. She returned quickly, rattling an armful of silver bracelets invitingly. She showed all her teeth.

"Straight up the stairs, dear. And watch your ankles," she finished obscurely.

A carpeted stairway climbed to the first story. The door at the top was open. He walked into a photographer's studio cluttered with professional furnishings. A couch after the style of Louis XVI; a barnacle-encrusted amphora; a section of white-painted trelliswork. A Leica camera screwed to a tripod was backed by a battery of arc- and spotlights. He stood in the middle of the studio, looking around uncertainly. A door that obviously led to the hall was bolted on the inside. A short man came out of another door marked PRIVATE. His black hair was combed forward over a glazed forehead. He wore green suede boots and a corduroy suit without pockets. His voice had a pronounced Welsh lilt.

"Come in, old man, come in!"

He kicked shrewdly at the charging Skye terrier, diverting its blind rush from Venner's legs. The animal's practiced swerve carried it far across the parquet flooring. It sniffed at a rug under the window then curled up, grumbling.

"Rascal," the man said censoriously. He stepped to one side, ushering Venner into the office. An old-fashioned desk was pushed against the inner wall. Piano-size montage of a girl in Bermuda shorts carrying a species of potted plant covered the other three walls.

"What can I do for you?" the photographer asked bluntly.

Venner cleared his throat. "Jerry Coughlin sent me. He suggested we might be able to do business together."

Emerson made an odd movement with his hand, mixing unseen salad in a bowl.

"Well, I'm always glad to meet a friend of Jerry's. How long have you known him?"

The interview was starting as negatively as Coughlin had warned it would. An introduction at this level demanded certain protocol. A member's standing in the milieu went unquestioned but a framework of reference was still necessary. There was no need to relate his twice-successful defense of Coughlin's brother. Emerson would have been given other and less specific recommendations.

"About six years," he said easily.

"Ahah." Emerson settled himself comfortably in his

chair. "I hear you're in the con business. What's your particular trouble?"

Venner's answer was to the point. "A passport."

Emerson released a dry smile. "I didn't imagine you came here to have your picture taken — or to buy books. What sort of passport and why?"

"It's for a partner of mine," Venner explained. "He's been having a little trouble with the law and needs to blow. There's no question of him using his own passport. We've managed to get hold of another one for him. But it needs some work done on it. Jerry tells me you do a foolproof job."

Emerson picked his teeth with a dead match, interested in what he found.

"I do," he said confidentially. "But it costs money. Did Jerry give you any idea how *much* money?"

Venner smiled. He'd defended enough thieves to know how to make the right assumption of indifference.

"He didn't say. There's plenty of money in the kitty."

"Two hundred and fifty quid, including outside expenses." Emerson looked at the ceiling.

Venner frowned. There was an implication that others would be in the know. His scheme depended on secrecy. It also depended on a forged passport that would stand minute inspection.

"The owner of the passport's on our side. As far as he's concerned, he isn't even going to know that the thing's missing. He's given up traveling himself for a while."

Emerson nodded. He pulled a drawer and threw a passport across the desk to Venner. It was his own. He followed it up with a magnifying glass.

"Take a good look at that picture—especially the Foreign Office stamp."

Venner brought the image into focus. The raised impression extended over the edge of the photograph, cutting into the page itself. Emerson covered his picture with his hand.

"Now look! Notice what's left — the word 'Foreign' and most of the lion. 'Office' and the unicorn are completely missing. The trick is to match these halves precisely so that the new picture'll stand up under a microscope if necessary. OK — we'll assume that's been done. Your friend Mr. Smith is sitting in some dump abroad minding his own business. Suddenly he gets involved in a punch-up with a drunk. Somebody calls the law. Smith's a foreigner — the first thing they do is ask for his passport. Then what?"

Venner explored the edge of his lip with his tongue. "How the hell should I know? Didn't you just say that the passport would stand up under the microscope?"

Emerson grinned in superior fashion. "I did. But suppose Smith talks back to the law. It doesn't even have to be that. Nobody knows what goes on inside a cop's head. This one might happen to dislike all foreigners. We'll assume that Smith's passport goes back to London for verification. Someone pulls the file on the original application and surprise, surprise. It's not Smith's picture and it's not his handwriting." He pantomimed a lavatory chain being pulled.

Venner was suddenly apprehensive. Though the chance would be one in a thousand, he couldn't afford to take it.

"What you're saying then is that the passport's of no real use — is that it?"

Emerson shrugged. "Jerry wouldn't have sent you here unless you carried some weight — I don't deal with spivs. I'm assuming your friend wants real protection. If you'll listen, I'll show you how he gets it."

"I'm listening," Venner said pointedly.

Emerson smoothed his hair forward. "You're talking to the one man in England who can help you. The price is high but the service is good. All you have to do is bring the passport and a couple of pictures of your partner. One of them will find its way into the Smith file at the Passport Office — never mind how — that's what I mean by 'outside expenses.' "

Venner was doubtful. The photographer's explanation was too detailed for comfort. His passport had been renewed. There'd be a ten-year-old photograph of him on file with his original application — the discrepancy in age would be obvious. He said as much to Emerson.

The photographer took the objection in his stride.

"Look, chum, you're paying for all that. I want an application for a passport and a renewal form completed in the real owner's name — in Smith's handwriting. By the time I've finished with his pictures, the original will *be* ten years old. The whole file is switched — do you get it?"

Coughlin's claim had been definite. "Don't take any

notice of the boots and all the Chelsea getup. Willy's
pricy but he's got the right gear and he's dead-reliable.
There's a lot of people who'd still be eating porridge if
it hadn't been for Willy. Another thing — I've known
him fifteen years but you can bet he won't even tell me
the color of the tie you wore."

In spite of it all, Venner had no intention of identifying himself with the passport.

"The owner's picture's already been removed," he
said casually. "For obvious reasons."

Emerson turned the corners of his mouth down, looking at Venner closely.

"His name's still on it, isn't it?"

Venner made no answer. The photographer shrugged.

"Suit yourself. It's none of my business but I'd better
show you something just in case the picture *hasn't* been
taken off."

He left the room. Venner heard the dog patter after
him, the bolts on the hall door being withdrawn. It was
five minutes before Emerson returned, having re-
fastened the outer door. He was carrying what looked
like a small juice press. He put it on the desk and
gummed a glossy print on a piece of paper. His hands
worked skillfully, fitting picture and paper beneath
the head of the press. He clouted the lever and gave the
result to Venner. The reproduction of the Foreign Office
stamp was perfect. Emerson carefully lifted a corner of
the photograph. He swabbed under it gently, using a
fine-haired brush dipped in spirit. After a while the
picture came away cleanly from the backing paper. He
recorked the bottle of spirit and wrapped it with the

brush in paper. He handed the package to Venner.

"I don't give a bugger *whose* picture's on the passport," he said. "Just be careful how it's taken off. You saw what I did. Dissolve the bond of gum — don't tear it. OK?"

Venner opened his briefcase and produced a typewritten piece of paper.

"I need this reproduced on hospital stationery with a couple of X-ray pictures to back it up. Can you do that?"

Emerson read the typescript, square eyebrows lifted.

"The best of British luck to him whoever he is. Will Guy's Hospital do all right — there's some of their paper about somewhere?"

"Perfect." Venner's voice was steady. "It's important that the name's spelled correctly."

Emerson checked the sheet indifferently. "Stephen Venner? OK. The X-ray photographs will cost you another tenner — I'll have them here in two days." Clearly the name meant nothing to him.

Venner shifted his feet. The circumstances of his assumed death were bound to make headlines in the national press. His passport described him as a solicitor. Emerson would be certain to recall the combination of name and profession. The photographer would know that he'd forged a passport for a man now dead. A character as cagey as Emerson would do his best to forget the whole transaction.

Venner stood up. "I'll come back in a couple of days, then. Have the other stuff ready when I bring the passport."

"Don't forget the cash." Emerson smiled. "Nice

clean loot that I can pay into my bank and not feel embarrassed. You'd be surprised what some of the boys
have brought in — fivers looking as if they've been kept
in a case of haddock — and smell like it. Give me a ring
about an hour before you're coming. There's never anything on the premises."

Venner nodded. "If I'm meant to use the back stairs
again, you'd better tell matron."

"You don't have to worry about Gloriana," Emerson
said fondly. "The only thing she hates more than a copper is two of them. She was married to one for twenty-
five years."

The terrier bared its teeth as Venner crossed the
studio. Emerson stood at the head of the stairs, hand
lifted in the thieves' traditional farewell.

"Be lucky!"

It was past four by the time Venner had finished in the
City, five before he reached Kingston Hill. He put his
car away and walked through the hedge to the kitchen
entrance. A gray-haired woman with a prune mouth
was gathering clothes from a line slung across the yard.
She pinned the double armful of linen with her chin,
speaking with difficulty.

"If it's Mrs. Venner you're looking for, sir, she's resting
in the garden. She's not feeling well."

He went through the kitchen into the house. Mrs.
Collins' guarded hostility stemmed from her devotion
to her mistress. Her life was a completely vicarious one
in which Venner figured as archvillain. She was as
irritating and irreplaceable as creaking house foundations. He locked his briefcase away in the library and

sat for a while at his desk, thinking about die stamps. MacLaren's passport would be Canadian. Even so, the system used to frank the photograph would correspond to that used by the British. Emerson's demonstration had given him an idea. If he could switch his own picture for MacLaren's on the Canadian passport, the exchange of identities would be complete. Any attempt to have the requisite embossing machine made in England would be asking for trouble. But in Spain there'd be die makers — qualified men whose interest in a foreign symbol would be negligible.

He strolled out to the terrace. A round-shouldered man crouched on his heels, syringing a rosebush. He nodded greeting, the deep lines in his face filled with sweat. His slow West country speech was for the most part incomprehensible. "I've a mind to cut 'er right back. The afies is worrying 'er, drat 'em."

Venner smiled absently, looking across the lawn. Emma was sitting in a deck chair under the sycamores. He walked over to her. She opened her eyes as he touched her shoulder.

"I've found him," he said quietly.

She passed a hand across her forehead and sat up. Her yellow shirt matched her shorts. There was an empty cigarette package on the ground at her feet — a phial of aspirins and a glass of water next to it.

"Found who?" She said in a puzzled voice.

He sat on the grass beside her. "The man I was looking for. A Canadian up on a drunk charge. Everything about him's right. Age — general description. Even the hair's more or less the same color."

"Where did all this happen?" she asked slowly.

Her manner was beginning to irritate him. "West London Police Court. The magistrate put him back for sentence. He'll be free tomorrow morning. He's homeless and my guess is that he's without friends. The probation report will tell us all that. Well — aren't you going to say anything?"

She opened her eyes. "Congratulations!"

His chin lifted. "I see — it's like that, is it. For the last few days we've been living a telephone call away from ruin. I find the one man who can get us out of trouble and you react as if I'd brought back the right brand of sausages!"

She looked at him thoughtfully. "It's amazing how emotional you can become about yourself, Stephen. What do you suppose the last few days have meant to *me* — or doesn't that matter? You know, you've had good value for your money all these years. I haven't slept with your friends. I've smiled at the right time and patted heads at gymkhanas. In fact, I created a public image of respectability for us out of *nothing*. What's more, I maintained it in spite of anything that you managed to do. Suddenly I'm told that it's all been a waste of time. Either I enter into a conspiracy to kill someone I never heard of or resign myself to selling underclothes for a living."

"Keep going," he said grimly. "I'm waiting to hear about the rest of your high, moral principles."

Her gaze settled on the blaze of color where the gardener was working. "I told you the other day how I felt. It won't stop me doing my share. I just don't want to talk about it. You talk too much. That's one of the things that worries me. That and this colossal conceit that dismisses everybody else but Stephen Venner as complete idiots."

He leaned back on his elbows. "What are you sniping at now? You think the Annesleys have outsmarted me, do you?"

"Not as much as you outsmart yourself," she said imperturbably. "You're your own hero all the time. These hard-core criminal friends you boast about — do you think they'd protect you if they knew you were implicating them in murder? This man with the passport, for instance?"

He shook his head. "In spite of whatever you think, I respect your judgment. But that's the sort of criticism that gets us nowhere. These people are loyal by necessity, Emma. There's something else — they're realists — they judge by results. I've a certain reputation among them."

She sounded anything but convinced. "How about your reputation with the people you've defended and lost — the ones who went to jail, or are you careful who you ask for help?"

He smiled up at her. "That's exactly it. I'm careful."

She pondered her answer for a while. "It's a strange thing, I don't think you're capable of doing anything by yourself, Stephen. If I'd understood that earlier, there'd have been no debts — no blackmail."

He laid his head back on the grass. "Ah, let's not go on with it. You'll find out I'm not the fool you take me for. By the way, I spent an hour with Purcell, this afternoon. The bank's putting up another five thousand pounds."

She looked down at him sharply. "I thought you said you'd reached your limit?"

"I did," he said lightly. "Actually, I borrowed the money on Heronscourt."

Rage flared on her face. "You must be completely mad. If everything else failed it's at least a roof over our heads."

"Over *your* head," he corrected. "I'd probably be in jail. I had to have the money, Emma. We've got to convince this man MacLaren of more than just his safety. Have you ever *seen* five thousand pounds spread out on a table. It answers an awful lot of questions."

She refused the image, stony-faced. "Miss Shepherd telephoned. The house agents have sent another batch of photographs of the island. She wants to know what to do with them."

He got up stiffly, dusting the dirt from his trousers.

"I'll collect them in the morning. Why don't we have dinner out for once? I dunno — we might even pretend to like one another for the evening."

She chased an aspirin with the last of the water.

"I can think of nothing I'd like less. I can't imagine how I've been able to stand you for seventeen years."

Ross MacLaren — Thursday 2 July – Friday 3 July 1964

I<small>T WAS</small> the fat jailer who opened the cell door — the witty one.

"Right," he said. "Pick up your parrots and monkeys. Nobody aboard ship without a jockstrap."

MacLaren killed the last of Wilbraham's cigarettes and came to his feet. The young cop who had arrested him was waiting in the passage. He escorted MacLaren into court. The scene was enlivened by a group of police cadets, attentive to their instructor. The people in the front row of the public gallery nudged, hawked and coughed. There was a change in the press box. Yesterday's bored beginner had been replaced by an older man. MacLaren recognized the hard-eyed stare of a *Globe* reporter. The hatchet was going to be sunk a couple of inches deeper. He would probably make the HUMAN TRAGEDY column in some butterfudge treatment of the evils of drink. Wilbraham was sitting behind the reporter, staring blankly at the wall.

Werner's entrance was made briskly. The polka-dotted

bow tie he was wearing gave him an improbable appearance of abandon. The clerk made his announcement as
if it were hot news.

"This man was remanded for sentence, sir. I am told
that the probation officer has completed his report."

Werner nodded into the heel of his hand. "Ah yes. I
realize that this was at short notice, Mr. Wilbraham.
Did you find anything at all likely to help us?"

Wilbraham came up like a hippopotamus surfacing.
He licked the crusted bismuth from the edges of his
mouth.

"Not very much, I'm afraid, sir. MacLaren is forty-
four years old and was born in Bruce County, Ontario.
I understand that his father farmed there on a fairly
large scale. He went to school in Toronto and then
straight from university into the army. His service record is excellent. In 1945 he was demobilized with the
rank of captain and came back to this country a couple
of years afterwards. His first job in England was on the
reporting staff of the *Daily Globe*. He continued to work
for this newspaper, becoming chief crime reporter in
1953. In 1956 he was dismissed after a dispute with the
Board of Directors."

The man in the press box looked up, his tight smile
ironical. Werner repeated the words with misgiving.

"A dispute about what — his drinking habits?"

Wilbraham changed legs. "I'm afraid I can't give you
any proper information about that, sir. No one I talked
to at the *Globe* offices seems to know. What *is* certain is
that MacLaren was only dismissed after a full inquiry

had been made into his grievances. The present editor describes MacLaren's attitude as high-handed and disloyal."

Werner brooded. MacLaren wiped his hands surreptitiously on his trousers.

"Go on," said the magistrate.

"Since then he's had a number of jobs," Wilbraham continued. "Most of them the door-to-door salesman type. In his own words he's become a drifter with no sense of responsibility to anyone or anything. He's out of work at the moment and tells me he has no relatives living and no friends."

Werner settled himself on his forearms. "This report confirms my own impression of you, MacLaren. You're the sort of chap who confuses liberty with license. One can sometimes feel a certain amount of sympathy with the man who is out of step with society. Not in your case. You didn't start in the gutter — you found your way there deliberately. This makes your twelfth appearance in a court for the same offense — drunkenness. I suppose you'd like me to fine you — a cozy arrangemnt that leaves you free to go out and do exactly the same thing all over again."

MacLaren stood at watchful attention and said nothing. Werner slewed round towards the probation officer.

"Where's he living, Mr. Wilbraham?"

Wilbraham looked at MacLaren for the first time. His eyes warned the Canadian.

"Nowhere, sir. He tells me he was unable to pay the

rent at his last place of lodging. I've managed to arrange temporary accommodation at the Watchtower Mission. But I'm afraid that's limited to two weeks."

Werner bent over and whispered. His clerk nodded agreement. The magistrate's face brightened.

"I'm quite certain that nothing I could do or say would alter your dependence on alcohol, MacLaren. I'm not even going to fine you. Before you start congratulating yourself, I want you to listen to me very carefully. I'm binding you over to keep the peace for twelve months. That means that if you come before the court during this period — *any* court — it's my opinion that you could be prosecuted under the Rogues and Vagabonds Act. I am marking your papers accordingly."

MacLaren ducked his head and left the dock quickly. He was halfway to the street when someone came up from behind. The cop who had arrested him was grinning.

"Hold it, mate, the pubs aren't open yet."

MacLaren removed the man's hand from his sleeve. "Maybe not. But we *are* out of school. Get lost."

The cop's geniality faded. "You're wanted by the probation officer. And you know something — you've just been bound over to keep the peace for a year. I've got an idea you're going to find it difficult as long as you stay in this neighborhood."

Wilbraham's office was a sparsely furnished room smelling of stale tobacco smoke. The probation officer closed the door.

"Sign these papers, Mac. You were lucky, I had hell's own job talking him out of remanding you for a full medical report. If you've any sense at all left, you'll re-move yourself from London as quickly as you can."

MacLaren pushed the documents back across the desk.

"I'm getting the signal from all over. But nobody says where or how."

Wilbraham rapped himself hard under the breast-bone. He shook with the force of the belch.

"The people in Canada House seem to think you ought to go home. In fact they told me your fare would be paid."

MacLaren smiled carefully. "I don't think they like me the way you do. Where's the Watchtower Mission?"

"Wavertree Road," said Wilbraham. "Shepherds' Bush. Ask for Brother Scobey. And lock your door if you drink. Don't forget — *Brother* Scobey. So long and good luck."

It was late afternoon. MacLaren was lying on the bed, his head to the door, a bottle of beer perched on his bare stomach. The cubicle walls and doors were made of mustard-colored boarding, eight feet high. A stout iron grille overhead discouraged extracellular curiosity. There was enough space for a bed, a chair and a foot locker. The cubicles were private in the sense that the doors had two inside bolts. MacLaren's clothes were hanging by the window he shared with his neighbor. Whitewash on the bottom panes prevented any affront to public decency.

He grabbed the beer bottle and emptied it without moving from the horizontal. Then he fumbled under the bed and covered the bottle with the chamber pot. The church clock across the road struck four times. The impact of beer on cold cottage pie made his belly queasy. The Mission catered for men who worked or looked for work. Meals, Brother Scobey had said, meant breakfast and supper. But MacLaren was to be fed because the first day was always difficult. Lunch was a slice of the evening's precooked meal eaten alone in the dining hall. The walls were hung with militant exhortations to resist the Devil and his works. When he'd eaten he'd carried his tray to the serving hatch. The inmate-cook's hoarse whisper had a note of hopelessness, as though he found his own suggestion implausible.

"Slip it over 'ere when Scobey's back's turned. I'll take care of it for yer."

The lone bottle of beer in MacLaren's pocket had seemed to emit sound signals.

He rolled over on his stomach. The rough sheets were clean and the high-ceilinged room reeked of carbolic. There was an impression of seediness more hopeless than any squalor. It was here that the last-ditch stands in defense of respectability were staged. Shirts stuck to walls ironed themselves dry, mattresses left a crease and a pattern of besprings on shabby trousers.

He reached across, putting a firm thumb on the bolt as he heard the approaching footsteps. Brother Scobey's voice was a blend of cheer and suspicion.

"Brother MacLaren?"

He imagined the nose flairing contraband. Two weeks, he thought suddenly. Christ no, not even two days. He withdrew the bolt and let the cubicle door swing inward.

Brother Scobey's hair burst from his scalp like a forced growth. He looked primly away from MacLaren's nakedness, fastening his gaze on the cigarette butts in the Canadian's shoe. His smile indicated some experience of indiscretion.

"Rules are rules, Brother, we must obey them. There's somebody downstairs to see you."

MacLaren stayed where he was. The possibilities were limited. It could only be Wilbraham or that bastard from the *Globe.*

"When you say 'somebody,'" he asked, "which do you mean — a character sprinkled with dandruff or a paddle-headed prick from the press?"

Brother Scobey winced. "A lady. And if I were you I'd wash my mouth out before I spoke to her."

MacLaren swung his feet to the floor and pulled on his trousers. He gently massaged the congealed horror of meat and potatoes in his middle.

"Either you're drunk or she is. I don't know any ladies."

Brother Scobey scored easily. "I can believe that. But she's asked for you by name."

MacLaren found his shirt. "I'll be down in a couple of minutes. Show her round the stables and make sure she doesn't get kicked." He shut the door firmly in the other's face.

When he heard the man's step on the stone stairs, MacLaren padded in stockinged feet as far as the washroom. He lifted the iron cover and dropped the beer bottle into the cistern. Standing in front of the cracked glass, he combed some sort of order into his gray hair.

The police-station razor blade had skipped the stubble in the cleft of his chin. His shirt was doing duty for the third day running. But at least the cut of the jacket defied age and rough treatment. He scrubbed at his front teeth with the end of a match.

He saw his visitor before he reached the bottom of the stairs. She was standing facing the street, copper-haired and cool in a white sharkskin shift cut like a toga. She turned and came to meet him, her hand outstretched. A heavy bracelet of Milanese mesh encircled her right wrist.

"Mr. Ross MacLaren?"

He gave her anything between thirty and forty. Her tone and manner accepted him as an equal. It had been a long time.

"That's right," he said awkwardly.

She lowered her voice, flicking her eyes across the hall. Brother Scobey was still lurking as though he had some proprietorial interest in the interview.

"We can't very well talk here. I have a car outside."

He lifted his shoulders. "Wherever you say."

He slumped in the red leather bucket seat, watching her brown, capable hands spin the Sprite eastward. She drove well, using the small car's acceleration to get her out of trouble, her foot easy on the brake pedal. The bonework of her face was unblurred, her mouth on the large side. Man picked up by beautiful woman in convertible. The zenith of male wishful thinking, he told himself. She gunned through changing traffic signals and into the park. Half a mile along the South Carriageway she pulled over to the curb. She lit a cigarette and sat for a moment, looking at him speculatively. He noted the initials on the gold lighter. E.V. The sun was warm on his shoulders. He watched an afternoon ride trot along the Row, led by a diminutive girl on a gray pony.

"You're wondering what this is all about?" she asked suddenly.

"In a general, uncomplaining sort of way," he replied. She pulled a copy of the *Globe* from her white straw bag, folded it at an inner page and passed the newspaper to him. A two-column feature was headed by a bold banner.

MAGISTRATE'S WARNING TO EX-REPORTER

He read on. The facts had been woven into a moral piece about the evil of a man's dependence on drink. He returned the paper without comment.

She pushed the hair out of her eyes. "That's how I knew where you were living."

"You must have been in a hurry," he observed. "This edition couldn't have been on sale for more than three-quarters of an hour."

Her color heightened. "I *was* in a hurry. I kept thinking that you'd get out of that place as soon as you could. I wanted to get hold of you before that happened. I have a proposition that might be of interest to you."

He watched her expression closely without finding the hint he needed.

"If you're saving souls," he said at last, "you just rang the wrong doorbell."

Her look suggested a growing impatience. "You're making yourself ridiculous, not me."

He cocked his head at her. "Am I? You know, you're completely out of character. They usually wear home-spun stockings and six rows of hand-carved beads. What it all adds up to is a hard day's work on the woodpile in exchange for lettuce sandwiches and their girlhood reminiscences. You're certainly different but the answer's still no, Thanks for the ride." He made as if to unfasten the latch of the door.

She moved quickly to stop him, her voice sharp with frustration.

"Don't make things more difficult for me than they already are. *Please* don't. I'm desperate, Mr. MacLaren. I need help and I'm willing to pay for it."

Her vehemence sobered him. "Help — what sort of help?"

"Won't you shut the door?" she pleaded. He did so. "I need your courage and your intelligence," she said quietly.

The intensity of her manner made him uneasy. It would be just his luck to be hooked up with some sort of head case. It was necessary to create an atmosphere of understanding.

"Where do you live?" he asked cautiously.

She shook her head at him, taking a deep breath. "Dear God! That really seems to be it, doesn't it. You're telling yourself you've got a lunatic on your hands, aren't you?"

He temporized. "We've all got troubles — yours are probably less tough than you imagine."

She seemed on the verge of the outburst he dreaded. She controlled herself with an effort.

"I see. What a fool I am. I'm sorry, Mr. MacLaren. Would you like me to drive you back or would you rather walk?"

He looked at her again and revised his opinion.

"Neither. But I'd feel a whole lot easier if I knew exactly what it is you want from me."

The pulse jumped in her brown throat. She leaned towards him, the transformation complete.

"Suppose someone paid you to break the law — paid you well — would you do it?"

The way she posed the question committed her to nothing — not even an opinion. He stared at her for a while.

"I've got *all* the vices," he said finally. "How about yourself?"

She spoke like a woman in trouble. "Please answer me."

He shrugged. "There are three sorts of crimes. Crime against the State — crime against property and crime against the person. Since I'm not a patriot, I've no views on treason. I wouldn't steal your handbag for a variety of reasons — none of them particularly ethical. And during the war I did my best to knock off an assembly of complete strangers. I never stopped to ask whether they objected. Is there anything in all that that's of use to you?"

She turned her wrist, glancing at a white-enameled watch. "You know what I think — that we ought to have dinner together. To put your mind at rest — I'm not suffering from delusions and I'm not a nymphomaniac. Would you do that — I mean have dinner with me?"

He nibbled a fingernail, studying her face. She gave him look for look as if the invitation were essentially conventional. He broke first, grinning. Stretching out his foot, he jiggled the broken toecap.

"There's only one place where they'd let me in dressed like this. Fred's Cozy Dining Rooms. You wouldn't like the food or the customers."

She switched on the ignition, watching the flickering gauge-needles.

"I'd already thought of that," she answered casually. "I propose to buy you some clothes. I hope that at least you'll hear me out. If your answer's no — the clothes are a gift. Entirely without strings."

He fastened his seat belt. "You just got yourself a customer."

She rounded Hans Crescent and bleeped her horn twice. The doorman moved a NO PARKING sign so that she could angle the Sprite to the curb. She led the way into the department store. In Menswear, she lost no time cutting out the manager from his acolytes. She spoke very clearly.

"This gentleman would like to see some clothes. When he has made a selection, he will want to change. You'll give the bills to me."

The manager added inches to his height and summoned an assistant.

"Thank you, madam. Accompany the gentlemen, Reeves."

MacLaren shopped from counter to counter. She'd find he played this game as well as she did. He chose a dark blue suit of Italian silk, half a dozen shirts, fine-meshed underwear and a pair of featherweight shoes. He changed clothes in a fitting room. He tucked a handkerchief into place and took a look at himself in the long mirror. He dumped his last misgiving with the pile of discarded clothing and walked out to her. She rounded her mouth, her eyes approving.

"Some sort of light coat, don't you think?"

"Oh, I don't know — I don't think it looks like rain," he said smoothly.

The manager moved on invisible roller skates, fluttering the collection of bills in his hand.

"Are you charging this, madam?"

She answered quickly. "No — I'll pay cash." She counted the money from a pigskin wallet. The initials E.V. were gold-leafed across one corner. MacLaren's impression was that she was known in the store. He followed her out, the package of spare shirts under his arm. She opened her car. He stood, unsure what the next move was meant to be. She swiveled the driving mirror, touched her mouth with red and rolled one lip over the other.

"It's almost six. I didn't realize it was so late. What do you suggest as an alternative to . . . what was the name of the place?"

"Fred's Cozy Dining Rooms. I'm a little out of practice. I'll leave it to you."

"The Ritz," she decided. "It's quiet. Perhaps you'll book a table for eight-thirty. I'll meet you downstairs."

He felt the crinkle of bank notes as he took her outstretched hand. She drove off towards the river. He was unlikely to forget the number on the license tag — CIK

220. He was suddenly aware of the doorman's curiosity and walked round the corner. He opened his palm on four five-pound notes. His father's gentle irony was somehow very apt at this moment. *Fantasy's where you find it, like apple scab, only a whole lot more use. The trick is to play it to the hilt and then be done with it.*

He strolled in the direction she had taken, pausing at the corner of Pont Street to buy a flower for his buttonhole. Three blocks south, he turned into a small hotel. The décor inside was subdued and expensive. A wall bracket in the form of Bacchus pointed to the bar. MacLaren stood at the hall porter's desk, turning the pages of a newspaper. He offered his profile deliberately to the clerk behind the reception desk. The mirror showed the man's hand drop below the level of the counter. That would be the bell push. He dropped the newspaper, timing himself to pass the office door as it opened. He came to a halt, blocking the manager's urgent sortie.

"Mr. Santarelli!"

The baldheaded man held his ground. His dark eyes showed wary recognition.

"You remember me, surely," said MacLaren. "About a year ago. You had me thrown out of this establishment on the pretext that I took off my shoes and went to sleep in a chair."

A matron with mauve hair lowered her book and inspected them severely. Santarelli retreated into his office.

"Would you mind coming in here, please?"

MacLaren took the straightbacked chair. A teletype machine clicked beyond the ground glass separating the manager's office from the reception desk. Over the years, he'd been bounced from better places and worse. The Rivage was no more than a symbol. Chance had designated it as the scene of his exorcism. Chance and the memory of a foot planted heavily in his rear end.

The hotel manager started a cagey explanation.

"It's coming back to me now. People were complaining about your behavior and it was past midnight. I do my best to run this hotel without trouble. But I have a duty towards my guests. The hall porter assisted you off the premises."

MacLaren admired the brilliance of his new shoes.

" 'Assisted' me's the understatement of the year. I'd been drinking in the bar for four hours. Why couldn't he have assisted me into a cab, for instance? Instead of giving me a flying start out on the street, then calling the cops?"

Santarelli wriggled his shoulders. "I've no idea whose instructions he was acting on — certainly not mine. You haven't come here to create a disturbance, I hope?" His voice was loud enough to be heard next door. The receptionist's shadow moved discreetly across the glass.

MacLaren put the man's mind at rest. "Not in the least. I'd like to buy myself the best whisky sour in town. I happen to think you sell it. The formula avoids the inconsistency of an apology on either side."

The manager hid his eyes under thick lids and smiled with bogus geniality.

"That sounds like a sporting solution. Our bar is generous with quantity and quality. I hope you will continue to be satisfied with both."

MacLaren uncrossed his legs. "I'll leave you to the more dubious prospects. I'm sure of it."

He crossed the lounge, resolved that this would be the last time he set foot in the place. But for the moment, he was still armored in fantasy. A hundred pounds' worth of new clothing was powerful magic.

The bar was a decent place for drinking — curtained against the unhelpful light of day, with an absence of mirrors. The chairs were deep and welcoming. The lilac-jacketed barman turned on a professional smile.

"Good evening, sir, what'll it be?"

"Whisky sour," said MacLaren pleasantly. "Long on the scotch and short on the orange."

The man flourished his shaker with a pipe major's abandon. He set the heavy tumbler in front of Mac-Laren, his button eyes suddenly alert.

"Tell me if that's about right, sir."

MacLaren rested an elbow on polished teak and tilted the glass.

"Perfect," he decided. He dribbled a handful of salted nuts into his mouth and carried his drink to a table.

"I wonder if you'd call the Ritz. I'd like a table for two in the Grill Room. Eight-thirty. My name is Mac-Laren."

He rotated the chilled glass between his fingers, aware of the strength of the mixture. He'd have one more before dinner, no more. Sharpened hindsight re-created the woman's face and voice. She spent too much time on her appearance not to be conscious of the fact that the result was desirable. He had a feeling that she made the effort principally for herself. She wore a wedding ring and he figured her to be shrewd, determined and as tough as a ten-minute steak. He finished the rest of his drink and signaled the bar.

"I'll take the other half."

The barman carried over his tray. "That's all right about your table, Mr. MacLaren. Eight-thirty."

MacLaren spoke idly as the man made change for the five-pound note.

"You haven't said so but I'm sure you remember me."

The man stacked the coins dexterously. "Yes, I remember you, sir."

"How could you forget?" MacLaren smiled. "You used a very pretty half nelson on me that night. You ought to try it again some time. Now that I have feet on the ends of my legs."

The man's shoulder muscles bunched and relaxed.

"Yes, sir. Will that be all, sir?"

MacLaren pushed some change back at the man.

"Not quite. The most successful barman I ever met had a theory — he figured he'd be out of business without drunks, con men and kept women. Buy yourself a bottle of Miltown. You've got a long night ahead."

He took his time over the second drink and left the premises without looking back. The time by the post-office clock on Sloane Square was a quarter to eight. He crossed the street to the cab rank and climbed into the first hack. The upholstery smelled musty. He pulled down both windows, grateful for the breeze blowing through the fountain. The Fate Sisters were fickle. He was suddenly apprehensive. There were a million reasons why E.V. would not show for the date.

The driver turned round, his hand hovering on the meter flag.

"I ain't got all day, you know, mate. You want this cab or not?"

MacLaren started. "Sorry — the Ritz — Piccadilly entrance."

He left his parcel of shirts in the cloakroom and went downstairs. The bar was crowded. He stood in the door-way until he had located her. She was alone at a table, apparently oblivious to everything but what she was reading. The deceptively simple dress she wore made the most of her small hips and high breasts. Another woman might have rejected the velvet band as unsuit-able — worn the red-beech hair a little shorter. The aloof E.V. seemed above criticism. A debs party over-flowed from the bar, blocking the way to her table. He used his weight to shoulder past their escorts. The gen-eration mistook courtesy for weakness. She made a place for him on the seat beside her. Her quick smile looked as if she meant it.

"I've been wondering whether you really would come. I'm glad you did."

He watched the play of her well-kept hands. She wore a large emerald-cut brilliant on her engagement finger. She leaned, intimately close, taking the light he offered.

"Let's play this thing straight," he said pleasantly. "You knew I'd be here."

She shook her head. "I knew nothing of the sort. When I left you, you looked anything but convinced. Have you decided that I'm harmless?"

He said no to the waiter's enquiry. " 'Harmless' isn't the adjective that comes to mind," he added.

She was mock-disconsolate. "Oh dear. That sounds very critical. Are you quite sure you won't have a drink?"

He lifted his gaze from her firm thigh. "Right now I don't think I need one."

She picked up her bag. "Then we'd better eat. My drink's paid for. You see, I'm telling the truth — I wasn't at all sure you would be here."

This time, the group of youngsters made way for them. Compared to her, he thought, the girls were about as exciting as hysterical heifers. Up in the tall-ceilinged room, the maître d'hôtel found his name and table on the floor plan. They sat looking out across Green Park. Beyond the trees and water, the stepped silhouette of Westminster was bathed in violet light. Encouraged by her deference, he ordered melon, cold salmon and a bottle of Niersteiner. They ate slowly, his confidence growing with the influence of the hock and her attentiveness. He was being flattered and didn't care. He parried her occasional shrewd enquiry about his family with some generality or other. Once the coffee cups had been cleared, he drank Drambuie and bought himself a Larrañaga.

He cocked his head. "All right. Whose piggybank gets robbed?"

The waiters moved about them quietly, drawing curtains. Her eyes were remote in the soft light. She tilted her head over the pattern she was scratching on the tablecloth.

"This isn't going to be easy. It's not a pretty story. I'm not quite sure I know where to start."

"Try the beginning," he suggested dryly.

She made a sign of embarrassment. "Sometimes the end is best. I'll be quite frank with you. My husband's suffering from an incurable disease. He wants you to help him die."

He looked round guiltily. The loudness of her voice was in his mind. People at the other tables were totally absorbed in one another. The waiters stood like wax dummies against the wall. He cleared his throat disbelievingly.

"Have you got any idea what you're saying?"

She nodded. "Unfortunately yes. You said this afternoon that you had killed complete strangers during the war. I can at least give you an idea that makes more sense."

He flicked the ash from his cigar. "Is that right? It happens that the government and my commanding officer thoroughly approved of the scheme."

"Is that what you need — approval?" she interjected quickly.

"If it's the sort that stops me being hanged, you're damned right I need it," he answered.

She thought about this for a while. "I'm not sure that I understand you. I suppose the people you were trying to kill must have objected. My husband's *asking* you."

He leaned over the table, making his words tell. "I'm beginning to hear a loud rattling of chains in the background. I don't like it."

She moved restlessly. "I know. You don't have to tell me that I'm doing badly, Mr. MacLaren. I'm very conscious of it. I suppose there should be some special way for me to be looking and talking. But I can't laugh — I can't even cry any more. I'm sorry."

Her throat rose from shadowy hollows and the corner of her mouth was set with a small mole. He felt she was making no play at all for his sympathy. Because of it, he was suddenly sorry for her.

"Take it easy," he remonstrated. "All I'm trying to say is that you needn't waste time exploring my ethics. The way I see it, it's a crime to keep a cretinous child alive. Society says I'm wrong. If you want to go ahead and talk, I'm ready to listen."

She threw him a quick look of gratitude. "Thank you. I'm old enough not to be embarrassed by the truth. Like a lot of other women, I married for security — not affection. My husband's not a fool. Nor is he abnormal. What I was unable to give him, he tried to find elsewhere. Please don't think I'm being sorry for myself. All I'm trying to do is explain how things are between Stephen and me. I stopped worrying about it years ago. We have no children. The reasons for my staying with my husband have continued to be strictly selfish."

He put his glass down on the table. "You're not talking to your analyst — quit using me as a couch. I'm ready to believe everything you say about your marriage. What makes you say your husband's suffering from an incurable disease?"

Her mouth worked nervously. "Cancer of the stomach is no longer a matter of guesswork, that's why. He has three months to live at the outside. Possibly less."

He swirled the last amber drops and swallowed them.

"You're not making sense. All you need is a bottle of sleeping pills. If your husband's in pain — your doctor must be prescribing sedatives."

There was no one within earshot but she pitched her voice lower.

"Does this make more sense — everything we own has been mortgaged to the hilt. The only thing Stephen has to leave is the proceeds of a life-insurance policy. You must know about life insurance and suicide. Getting hold of you is his idea — not mine. He's willing to pay you five thousand pounds."

"Jesus God!" he said fervently. "How many nuts have you tried to peddle this idea to already?"

One of her hands was a vise on the other. She started to say something, her eyes shut tight, then her voice broke. He pushed a cigarette into her fingers and held a match for her.

"What the hell are you crying for?" he asked. "I didn't yell 'police!' did I?"

"I'm not crying." She opened her eyes to prove her point. "I'm just desperate. I don't have any talent for this sort of thing. I must tell you the truth and the more I tell the less likely you are to help. Don't you *see* that?"

"Look," he said reasonably. "I don't know whether to

take you seriously or not. But if you're on the level, don't you realize the risks you're running?"

"I think so," she answered. "Some of them I've guarded against. The others . . ." Her hands were expressive.

Cigar smoke wreathed his face. He looked round the elegant room. A light burned serenely under a silver chafing dish — a symbol of what magazines called "gracious living." The surroundings were incongruous for a discussion of murder. And no matter how you looked at it, murder was what this woman was proposing. She might well be desperate but neither she nor her husband was stupid. They wanted a violent death and no post-mortem. The insurance company would meet its liability. An actuary would get busy with a slide rule and people in her husband's age group might pay a fraction of a cent more premium per annum.

"You said five thousand pounds?" he asked.

She nodded. "And no danger — not even to your conscience!"

The mixture of drinks was just beginning to hit him.

"You mean the small still voice that speaks in the night? I have a highly selective ear."

She glanced at him questioningly. "Are you saying yes?"

"Don't rush me," he warned. "I get nervous when I'm crowded." He caught the waiter's eye.

Her own voice was steady. "I must know one way or the other — tonight."

"Not tonight," he said. "Tomorrow. I need time to think."

She gathered her things and stood up. "Thank you for my dinner." Her expression revealed nothing but polite friendliness.

She stayed close to him on the way out to the street. High over the city, the moon tipped against a black velvet backdrop. They walked east on Jermyn Street. She was holding his arm, her weight hanging a little, the faint pressure of her fingers exciting. Her face betrayed no hint that she was aware of the contact. He pushed his hands deeper into his pockets, fingering what was left of the money she had given him. Her car was parked in a mews off Bury Street. She unlocked it and eased herself behind the driving wheel.

She looked up at him. "How will I know your decision?"

He leaned on the canvas top of the convertible. It sagged under his weight. He was neither drunk nor crazy, he decided. But at this point in time, in this cobbled street, lonelier than any man had the right to be.

"Shall I tell you something," he said suddenly. "I think you're a liar. Why you should bother, I don't know, but you're lying."

She slid back the catch on the door. "You'd better get in," she said quietly.

"That's what I'd better do," he agreed.

The sound of the slamming door echoed along the mews. The ensuing silence in the car made the ticking of the clock on the dash seem loud. He struck a match, fumbling in the glove compartment. It was completely empty.

"Well, how *about* that!" he said with interest. "No

operator's license — no old garage bills — not even a lipstick. What are you scared of?"

She lit another of her interminable cigarettes, her eyes somber in the flaring match flame.

"As things are, I don't think that's any of your business. You just called me a liar. I'd like to know why."

He tried to give sense to what was no more than a hunch.

"Your statements don't agree with the facts, that's why. Your husband's supposed to be penniless. It doesn't stop you from spending a hundred and twenty pounds on me since this afternoon. And half an hour ago, you promised me five thousand. Added to all that, you neither act nor dress like someone on her way to the poorhouse. In my book, this all adds up to some fancy brand of lying."

"It does, does it?" She thought for a while. "I told you earlier that we were mortgaged to the hilt. Do you know what it is to be blackmailed, Mr. MacLaren?"

"I've been in the newspaper business," he said briefly.

"My husband's been blackmailed for some time. That's where most of our money's gone. Don't get the wrong idea. We need your help — not your good opinion. I just don't like being called a liar without justification."

"Haven't you gone to the police?" he asked curiously.

She made a sound of disgust. "That's an odd question, coming from you. Do the police help a man face his friends? What good does a prosecution do except bring the whole rotten story into open court? We paid like anyone else. If I still look too prosperous, I'm sorry."

She said it in a way that took the edge from his assurance.

"Let me be the one to be sorry. I don't seem to have the touch any more. You understand that if I did come in it would only be after I'd seen your husband."

She opened the ventilator and threw her cigarette butt out to the street.

"Naturally. I'm not a complete idiot. You can see him any time you like."

She exchanged high heels for a pair of driving loafers. He opened his door. "I'll be in the park at noon. The same spot we were in this afternoon. All I'm promising is that I'll be there. What's your name?"

She looked at him steadily. "First or last?"

"Take your pick," he said.

"Emma." It was almost too quiet to be heard.

He smiled. "Goodnight, Emma."

A westbound bus dropped him at Shepherd's Bush Green. He ducked into the jungle of West Kensington. A light was burning in the Mission hallway. He looked through the glass door. An elderly man wearing a cloth cap was asleep on a chair. MacLaren thumbed the bell push. The old man started violently. He pushed painfully on his knees, lifting himself with an effort. He tottered over to the door and peered out uncertainly.

"Yes, mister?"

MacLaren eased by quickly. "I live here."

The old man's tone changed abruptly. "Then ring the dratted bell properly, can't you? And 'oo give yer permission to be out at this time o' night, I'd like to know. With men sleeping and all that. What's yer name?"

MacLaren took the old man by the shoulders and forced him down in his chair.

"Look," he said soothingly, "you're dreaming up far too many problems for yourself, Pop. Why don't you go back to sleep?"

He climbed the stone staircase and stood in the doorway of the darkened dormitory. The sour stale smell of the room repelled him. Taking off his shoes, he tiptoed as far as his cubicle. He undressed in silence and got into bed. Through the open window the moon silvered the street. His neighbors slept restlessly as if repose were a privilege of the affluent. Deadbeats, he thought, surrendering independence for a bed and a bowl of stew. And how far ahead of them was he! Almost certainly these bums would uphold the edicts of a society that rejected them. They'd be for Hiroshima and for locking up would-be suicides. Faced with his particular choice they'd run a mile, giving every reason but the real one — fear of consequence.

He was being asked "will you kill?" not "would you?" His mind whispered an answer without subterfuge. "If I'm safe, I will. He wants to die and I want to live."

He woke to the first quarreling chatter of the sparrows outside. He unlocked the door and slipped into the deserted washroom. The shock of cold water on his body left him breathless. He scrubbed his teeth, chose a clean shirt and went downstairs. Brother Scobey was at a table in the dining hall, cradling a mug of tea in both hands.

He inspected MacLaren's new clothes curiously but said nothing. MacLaren put a pound note on the table.

"I'm checking out. I guess this covers my stay here."

Scobey flinched — as if the source of the money were highly doubtful.

"I don't know. I think I'd have to see Brother Pearse — he's in charge and he's not up yet."

MacLaren pegged the note with the man's mug. "Tell him I said I was surprised at him."

Scobey looked back over his shoulder. The head behind the serving hatch vanished.

"Don't forget you've been bound over to keep the peace," he said in a loud whisper. "Mr. Wilbraham isn't going to like it."

"Just say I'm going to keep it somewhere else," MacLaren answered.

He took one last look at the framed admonitions to godliness and sobriety and walked out into the morning sunshine. Paint peeled on the shabby mansions, long-since converted to seedy communal living. Drawn curtains were still hostile to the light of day. A few cautious curs explored the garbage cans cluttering the dirty steps. He walked with quick determination — like a man leaving jail. A barber on Shepherd's Bush Green was opening his premises. MacLaren dropped into a chair and relaxed under hot towels. He kept his ears closed to the barber's profession of numerous opinions. The sliver of honed steel sang over MacLaren's jawline twice. He wiped his cheeks and used the man's comb. The barber was smiling into the glass over MacLaren's shoulder.

"You're wearing it a bit long, if I may say so, sir. Not

'with it' as the modern generation says. I could give you a new styling — it wouldn't take long."

MacLaren peered deep into the looking-glass. Sleep had washed the soreness from his eyes.

"Some other time," he promised. "When I'm feeling more modern."

He grabbed a hasty breakfast in an automat. Eight-thirty. Another half hour and the department store would be open. He rode the crowded subway as far as Knightsbridge and joined the rush of pedestrians. The first customers were already invading the entrances to the store. He cut through the Banking Hall and into Menswear. The manager was supervising a display of Italian sweaters. MacLaren strolled over to him.

"I wonder if I might have a word with you. I came in here yesterday afternoon."

The manager's recognition was immediate. "Of course, sir. I remember very clearly." He contemplated the drape of MacLaren's suit with approval.

MacLaren drew him aside with a gesture.

"This is a little embarrassing but I'm sure you'll understand. The lady I was in with thinks she dropped her charge card here. If it's found, there are good reasons for her not wanting it returned to her home. Is that quite clear?"

The manager slanted a look of complicity. "Perfectly, sir. If you'll take a seat, I'll make some enquiries." He tipped away then backtracked suddenly. "Would you be wanting to take the card with you, sir?"

MacLaren shook his head. "Not necessarily, no."

The manager frowned. "It's just that our rules are strict about charge cards. Unless you had a letter of authority from Mrs. Venner. Otherwise she'd have to collect the card herself."

MacLaren smiled easily. "Fair enough. She can pick it up next time she's in the store."

The manager was back in a few minutes. "There's nothing been handed in here, I'm afraid. In any case, Mrs. Venner paid cash. I've just checked the sales slips."

MacLaren got up. "It was just a chance. You know how women are — for all I know the thing's been found in another bag by now."

The man ducked his head. "Quite possibly, sir. I'm sorry I couldn't be of more help."

MacLaren loitered for a while at the sock counter. The manager's interest in him seemed dead. The man had gone directly back to his display of sweaters. MacLaren moved over to the escalator. Upstairs, he made change at the post-office counter and stepped into a phone booth. There was something satisfactory about making a call *to* the store *from* the store. He sank the button and asked for Accounts.

"This is Mr. Venner speaking. My wife seems to have lost her charge card. It's just possible that she might have dropped it in the store. She was in yesterday."

The girl's voice was clipped and efficient. "Is the account in your wife's name, sir?"

"As far as I recall, yes," said MacLaren. "That's *Emma* Venner."

There was a few second's wait. "Yes, I have it now, sir. A joint account, isn't it? No — I'm afraid there's no record of Mrs. Venner's card being found. Would you like us to put a stop on the account being used, sir?"

It was hot in the booth. He was beginning to sweat.

"Not for the moment, no. We haven't really looked everywhere. It's quite likely that it'll still turn up somewhere in the house. If it *should* be handed in, do you have our address in the country?"

The girl bettered anything he had hoped for.

"We have two addresses — c/o Venner & Venner, 79 King's Bench Walk, and Heronscourt, Kingston Hill, Surrey. Is that the one you mean?"

He smiled into the mouthpiece. "That's it. Thank you very much. I'll let you know what happens." He replaced the instrument, sticking a foot in the door as he searched the phone book. The entry was in bold type.

VENNER & VENNER SOLRS AND COMISSIONERS FOR OATHS
79 KING'S BENCH WALK E.C.4.

He went over to the post-office counter. Using the back of a telegram blank, he scribbled down both addresses. Venner's profession added to the likelihood of his wife's story. Anyone who had enough on a lawyer for blackmail had the inside track. The Law Society's method of dealing with its own transgressors was drastic. He rode the escalator down to the library floor. He checked his first source in the comprehensive Reference Section.

The Law List told him no more than the telephone book and he drew blank in the *Directory of Directors*. The entry in *Who's Who* was more helpful.

VENNER, Stephen Edward, M.C., born Surrey, 1917. e: Winchester, Trinity College, Oxford. m: Emma Jowett. Partner, Venner & Venner, Solicitors. Hon. Sec. Aldebourne Field Sports Society. Sports: Racing, tennis, sailing. Address: Heronscourt, Kingston Hill, Surrey. t: Kingston 1109

It was nine-thirty. He left the store by the Brompton Road entrance and walked to the subway station. A southbound train took him as far as the Temple. Here he braved the traffic on the Embankment to hang over the stone parapet, looking down at the brown swirl of the river. A high-bridged tug was ferrying a line of barges upstream towards Westminster. A dog lay asleep in the sun on top of the wheelhouse.

He watched his cigarette butt sink in the wash from the tug. In a few short months even the wharves on the south bank would be hidden at this time of the day. Lights in the warehouses would burn the clock round. Pedestrians trapped in the fogbound misery of November would walk the choking streets nervously, avoiding one another's eyes. As winter hardened, the bums would heave rocks through store windows and have themselves committed to jail. The rest of the shiftless either died off or somehow survived till spring.

He leaned against the wall, looking across the Embankment. Beyond the railed-off grass, King's Bench Walk came to a dead end. He'd been playing with the prospect of winter misery as a child does a tooth due for the dentist. Five thousand pounds bought a lot of mileage. Too bad if he broke the rules to get it. They weren't of his making.

Signals halted the east-west lines of traffic at the bridge. He took advantage of the lull to cross the street. Screened by the trees, he watched the length of King's

Bench Walk. It was a little after eleven when a car stopped outside 79. The driver was gray-haired, tall and well-groomed. He stood for a while by the car, his pose alert — as though he sensed the watcher behind the trees. Then he ran quickly up the steps and into the offices of Venner and Venner. Instinct told MacLaren that this was the man he had been waiting for.

He walked into the maze of lanes and passages south of Fleet Street. He chose a downstairs bar well off the press beat. He ordered iced lager in a tankard and drank it slowly. This was like old times. The watching and waiting, the bluffed information. He hailed a cab outside the granite extravagance of the *Globe* building. Cab, bus, subway, cab. The conveyance he picked was a sort of barometer of his confidence. Years ago, at the height of his war with the *Globe,* they'd called in the anonymous psychiatric writer they used for hatchet work. "The Hidden Springs of Failure" had only just avoided libel. The piece followed the career of an unnamed Commonwealth journalist, describing his behavior as " . . . ambivalent. A psychopath more dangerous potentially than any Soho hoodlum."

Bad writing, he recalled, and piss-poor psychology. To swing from joy to despair and back again was hardly remarkable.

The cab followed the river as far as Vauxhall Bridge, then turned into the meanness behind Victoria Station. MacLaren paid off his driver. The short street ran from corner pub to a blank wall backing a warehouse. Weeds flourished in dank airless corners. The mean stretch of pavement was labeled improbably — Play Street. He picked his way over last week's refuse to where a fly-blown card in the transom offered: LODGINGS FOR RE-SPECTABLE SINGLE MEN.

He swung the door knocker hard a couple of times. The noise bounced the length of the cul-de-sac. A woman pushed her head out of a second-story window opposite. She leaned forward perilously, her hair confined in a variety of ironmongery.

"Welcome 'ome, Canada! Welcome 'ome, dearie. I read what the sods done to you. Knock 'arder — 'e's only lurkin'. *Counting 'is bleedin' money!*" She yelled at an invisible audience.

MacLaren recognized a sociable bag from the corner bar. He thudded the knocker half a dozen times in quick succession. The door flew inward with unexpected veloc-ity. The man who opened it wore a cotton singlet that exposed a hairy navel. His trousers were tied with cord just below the bulge of his belly. He had a wedge-shaped head and artfully arranged hair. He leaned his elbows on the narrow passage walls and inspected MacLaren's appearance with obvious disbelief.

"Wot the 'ell do you want?" he asked belligerently.

The blowsy woman leaned out even more danger-ously, trying to see down into the house.

"Give 'im some stick, Canada. I'm yer witness if 'e starts any of 'is old larks."

MacLaren settled his weight evenly on the balls of his feet. Out of condition he might be but there was still enough left to topple this bladder of lard.

"I've come for my suitcase," he said shortly.

The man's head sank low into his neck. "Is that so.

And 'ow about the rent — is yer secretary bringing it rahnd?"

MacLaren opened his hand and showed the money there. "Just get the suitcase."

The landlord backed into the passage very slowly. He led the way over bare boards and downstairs to the basement. The atmosphere was fetid with the stink of mice. They spun in cages stacked against the wall, worked wheels and vanished into mazes. The room looked as if it had been furnished from the city dump. The man unfastened a couple of padlocks on a cupboard. He reached inside. A suitcase dangled from one of his fingers. He hoisted its weight contemptuously onto the table.

"I been wearing yer joolry," he grinned.

"You could stand some sort of decoration," answered MacLaren. He groped in the bag, his first thought for the musical box. He'd carried it too far to lose it in a dump like this. The machinery whirred as he lifted the inlaid lid. He wound the spring carefully, indifferent to the fat man's sneer.

He saw the big living room, bright with Christmas trappings. The tree his father had cut hung with presents. His parents, flushed with the heat from the apple logs, sharing his own excitement as steel tines picked out an old Scots air.

He shut the box, threw the package of shirts into the bag and dropped the money on the table. The landlord struggled the cash into a pocket in his waistband. He blinked malevolently.

"Them clothes don't make that much difference, chum. You're still a layabout ter me."

MacLaren looked at him steadily. "I always thought the heads on your bedbugs were hideous. Yours beats even theirs. One of these days someone's going to take time out and rearrange it for you."

The fat man's breathing became stertorous. His eyes were the only part of him to move. MacLaren felt them all the way to the street door, planted like icepicks in the middle of his back. The door slammed violently behind him. The woman was still at her window, shielding her face from the sun.

"I 'eard most of that, Canada. You knocked 'im bandy. Wait till I get me girdle on and I'll buy you a drink."

He lifted a hand, grinning up at her. "I'll take a rain-check on that one, Bella. I don't know that I'd trust myself with a girl like you right now, girdle or no girdle."

He carried his suitcase as far as Victoria Station and checked it in the baggage room. It was just short of noon when he cut through into the park, using the passage by the barracks. He saw the Sprite parked twenty yards away. The top was down and the car empty. He sat on the nearest bench and waited. Emma appeared from the direction of the trees. Tall, wearing a sleeveless candy-stripe dress, her eyes hidden behind dark glasses. She stopped in front of him, swinging her car keys.

He watched the movement of her hand warily, sensing her hostility. "Hi!" he said.

She put her keys into her handbag. "I don't like people who are too clever, Mr. MacLaren."

"Ross," he corrected. "It's easier."

She showed him the charge card in her hand. "I

thought you'd be glad to know this had never really been lost. They telephoned just before I left the house."

A dog trotted over, stiff-tailed, to kick the dust under the fat chestnut trees. A nursemaid hurried her charge past a couple, blatantly amorous on the grass. He threw his jacket over his shoulder and stood up.

"Let's you and I take a stroll," he suggested. They started walking slowly towards the shimmer of lake.

"It wasn't necessary," she said in a low voice. "You could have trusted me."

He shook his head. "Why should I trust *anybody?* What do you think this is — an invitation to a church bazaar?"

"Are you going to help us or not?" she asked quietly.

That she knew of his antics at the store irritated him less than her objections to them.

"I want to hear you before I answer that one. Sure, I've done my best to check you out. I'll go on doing it the best way I can. If there's anything you don't like about that, now's the time to say so."

She put her hand on his sleeve. "I'm sorry. You have every right to do what you did. Please help us, Ross."

The grass was still green underfoot. A city put its parks to strange uses. Each prosaic pursuit had its furtive shadow. Long-distance runners in training trotted by whores and birdwatchers. Doubtful bargains were struck on the benches overlooking grazing sheep and children at play.

"I'm in," he answered. "But I don't know that 'help' is the right word. I'm in for the cash — I need it."

She looked up at him, her face sober. "I can't tell you what you've just done for me. Suddenly I don't feel alone any more." She touched his sleeve lightly, taking her hand away as though doubtful of his approval.

He filed another mental reservation. She overworked the fluttering-finger bit.

They stopped on the bridge overlooking the Serpentine. Ducks cruised serenely on the water below, avoiding the erratic scullers.

"I'd better be on my way," he said after a while. "Two things — I want to meet your husband and I need more money. I'll look for a place this afternoon — somewhere I can start locking my own door for a change."

She counted another twenty pounds from her wallet. "There's an ice rink in Bayswater — it's a good place to meet. We'll be there at nine o'clock this evening."

He put the money in his pocket. "I'll be on time."

She took off her dark glasses, frowning. "I don't know what you expect Stephen to be like — it's difficult to explain. He tries not to be emotionally involved with what's happening. It's not always easy."

"Dying isn't," he said briefly. "However you do it. I'll see you at nine."

Emma Venner — Friday 3 July 1964

I т was three o'clock and lunch long over. She was sitting in the swing chair on the terrace. The chain overhead rattled as she pushed with her feet. The heady smell of carnation beds mixed with the freshness of watered grass. The long house lay silent in afternoon sunshine.

Her house, Emma thought with fierce jealousy. A place where she had fought the memory of an alien woman room by room till nothing remained of her.

Two things went together in her mind — hers by right of conquest. Heronscourt and her jewelry. The house had been mortgaged. She had no intention of letting Stephen get his hands on her trinkets. He had bought shrewdly over the years from a client in the secondhand diamond trade. She had been indifferent to the fact that each offering had been sparked by a guilty conscience.

She rubbed a little suntan oil where dark glasses had left the skin pale.

"We've talked everything to death except the future

of Heronscourt. For some reason or other you seem to avoid the topic."

Venner stirred in his chair. "Does it matter?"

She knew he was amusing himself at her expense.

"To me it does," she said in a level voice. "It's my house. You just happened to be born here."

He stretched out his leg, touching the sprinkler valve with his toes. A fine spray jetted over the lawn.

"You inherit my liabilities as well as my assets. It's up to you what happens to Heronscourt. I imagine you'd pay off the mortgage and go on living here. I'm sure Kingston Hill will be very touched. Frankly, I couldn't care less."

He shifted legs and sank deeper into the canvas-backed chair. At that angle, his resemblance to Mac-Laren was striking. Both had the same-shaped head, strong gray hair over dark eyebrows. Each man gave an impression of latent physical power. Above all, there was a projection of confidence common to them both — a hint of ruthlessness. She had a quick thought that she might have been underestimating her husband.

"I hope you're not proposing to deal with MacLaren on this cut-and-thrust basis. After this morning's experience we know what he's capable of. Just how are you going to maneuver him into giving you two passport photographs?"

Venner locked his hands behind his head. "You'll see. I knew what I was doing when I picked on him. Everything he's said and done so far is precisely what I would have expected from his background. The essential is that he has imagination."

"Isn't it possible that he has a little too much?" she suggested reflectively. "I've seen you make the same mistake before."

Venner smiled from a wealth of superior knowledge.

"Not this time, Emma. Five thousand pounds spread out over the table — you'll be able to see his mind go to work. You realize that we're going to have to use part of this money for working capital — that's unless you've got something hidden away in an old sock."

"I drew the last two hundred pounds from my account yesterday," she answered, "and most of it's already gone on him." She waited stonily for the suggestion that she might sell a little of her jewelry.

It never came. Venner yawned and flexed his shoulders.

"We'll bring him back here tonight," he decided, "and get it over with. The days are beginning to count."

The idea of the Canadian in her house disturbed her. She searched Venner's face for subterfuge. He nodded, bland and self-assured.

"You're at your best when things are going the way you want, Stephen. I'm worried what happens when they don't."

"That sounds a reasonable arrangement. I'll think and you worry. If you do your part as well as I'll do mine, we're home and dried. Try to remember that he's no threat at all as far as we're concerned. There isn't a single overt act we could be charged with at the moment. Not even conspiracy. The uncorroborated evidence of an accomplice isn't enough to secure a conviction. And Mac-Laren became part of a conspiracy when he met you in the park this morning. He can't go back — only deeper in."

"I hope you're right," she answered. "For both our sakes."

He blocked another yawn with his hand. "I thought I'd take a run over to Aldebourne this afternoon. There's a meeting of the gymkhana committee. I ought to be doing the things I usually do."

She pulled on her shoe. "I'd have thought that would be the last thing we needed."

He pulled a flower for his buttonhole. "Your wit's positively flashing today. I'll be back about dinnertime."

She waited till she heard his car roll onto the graveled driveway and then hurried. The bunch of keys was in the sock drawer of his dressing room. She used them to open the safe in the library. The interior was unusually crowded. The top shelf had been cleared of the various family documents. In their place were a large manila folder and a paper-wrapped package. Without looking inside she knew this would contain the mortgage money. She pulled out her jewel case and carried it over to the desk. She shut the door quietly and sat in her husband's chair. His indifference to her belongings was ominous. Stephen had no scruples when he needed money. He always mocked her use of the safe with stories about the ingenuity of professional thieves. He was quite capable at a time like this of walking off with everything she owned and selling it. Someone like Stephen would know how to stage a burglary afterwards. He might even have done it already.

She stared at the red leather case, steeling herself to lift the lid. The square-cut solitaire flashed reassuringly. She slipped the ring on her finger and opened one after another of the tiny boxes. Nothing was missing. The inch-wide diamond bracelet, the peacock clip, its resplendent feathers formed of sapphires, rubies and emeralds — everything was there. She packed each piece into a washleather bag, replaced the empty jewel case in the safe and locked up. She put the keys back in the drawer with a sense of triumph. He'd be too late now.

It was after four by the time she found parking space on the square behind Westminster School. She walked the rest of the way to Victoria Street. The display of jewelry in Gaynor's front window was discreet but elegant. Three generations of pawnbroking to the aristocracy had brought a certain distinction to the store's handling of the trade. She was suddenly nervous, certain that the strangers passing on the street knew why she was standing in front of the place. Three brass balls hung over the side entrance. As she pushed the door, a man hurried out, avoiding her glance. She whirled abruptly and went back to the front entrance. The shop interior was dark and hushed after the sun and bustle outside. A circular showcase held the center of the room. One diamond pendant was draped on a bed of dark blue velvet. A decorous assistant came to meet her. His grave expression, the impregnability of the massive safes against the wall, encouraged her.

"I have some jewelry with me — I would like to borrow some money on it."

The assistant's glance was positive and assessing.

"Of course, madam. Would you care to come this way?"

She sat facing him across a small table. He dribbled the contents of the washleather bag onto a piece of black cloth. His delicate fingers were mothlike. They touched the pieces of jewelry as though feel might determine value. He fitted a lens into his right eye and peered at the setting of her solitaire.

"You quite understand that there's no question of selling," she said defensively. "This is purely a temporary measure."

He nodded abstractedly as though he had heard the same thing many times. He set the solitaire on one side and examined the bracelet. Each piece was given the same meticulous inspection. He raised his eyebrow, catching the falling glass deftly in his palm. He wore a slightly puzzled expression.

"What sort of figure had you in mind, madam?"

She frowned. "The amount's of no real importance. All I really want is for these things to be in safekeeping."

The man's smile was polite and without offense.

"Then I think your bank would be of more use, madam. In any case we don't advance money on artificial jewelry."

She sat stiffly upright. "Did you say artificial jewelry?" She demanded coldly.

He spread his hands. "It's a generic term, madam. Strictly speaking the solitaire is a reconstructed stone, while the bracelet is white zircons. The colored stones are synthetic and the rest is paste. All the workmanship

is first class. In fact, if you wanted to sell, we might easily
be able to find a customer who'd be interested in the
collection as a curiosity. But I'd have to ask Mr. Gaynor
about that."

Her fingers curled protectively over her belongings.

"You don't know what you're talking about. My husband bought these from a client in Hatton Garden.
They're insured for fifteen thousand pounds."

The man sat with folded hands, his eyes sympathetic.

"I'm sorry, madam. I can assure you there's no possibility of a mistake. If you'd like a second opinion —
Mr. Gaynor is out at the moment but one of my col-
leagues . . ."

She swept the jewelry into her handbag with trem-
bling fingers.

"It doesn't matter," she said unsteadily. "Do you think
I might have some water, please?"

She sipped from the glass he brought her. He waited
solicitously until she rose.

"Can I get you a taxi, madam?"

She shook her head vehemently, no longer trusting
her voice. The street was a noise-filled canyon. Stephen's
face leered at her from shop windows, from the
crowded pavement, the tops of passing buses. She broke
into a half-run, stumbling on high heels till she reached
the locked car. She wrenched open the door and leaned
her forehead against the steering wheel.

A second opinion . . . the man had said it with the
contempt of an expert sure of his own judgment. She
was suddenly conscious of being trapped. First Heronscourt and now this! Everything that represented security

to her was sliding out of her grip. For the first time, she understood the hopelessness of her own position. The only place for her to go was where Stephen led. She switched on the motor. Once up on Wimbledon Common, she took the Portsmouth Road. She drove aimlessly in the hills beyond Leatherhead till the amethyst light began to fade in the woods. Venner was waiting on the front steps as she turned into the driveway.

His face was angry. "Where the hell have you been, Emma? It's after eight and we have to be there at nine. I've eaten already."

She walked towards him slowly. He had changed to a dark flannel suit with suede shoes and a club tie. This was the Surrey Sportsman. She knew every role he played, from Public Defender to Nightclub Romantic. Unhurriedly she transferred her bag from her right to her left hand. Then judging her distance, she struck him in the face as hard as she could.

He reacted swiftly. He caught her by the wrists and dragged her inside the hall. He kicked both doors shut. The imprint of her hand still flared on his cheek. He wiped his mouth carefully, inspecting his handkerchief for blood.

"Don't ever do that again if you know what's good for you," he said with quiet venom.

It took an effort to match his self-control. "It won't be necessary. I went to Gaynor's this afternoon. I just wanted you to know how contemptible I really think you are."

She emptied her handbag on the hall table. He bent down, collecting the scattered pieces of jewelry. She heard the safe door slam in the library and hurried after him. He was standing facing the window, shoulders squared, hands locked behind his back.

She lit a cigarette, disturbed but not frightened.

"Well?" She challenged.

He shrugged. "I'd let well alone if I were you. That jewelry isn't the less decorative because someone tells you it's artificial. We know how we feel about one another. We just can't afford dramatics."

Looking at him, she knew he was right. Their mutual hatred was less strong than the elemental fear of poverty and failure.

"There'll be no more," she promised. "I suppose we'd better go. I'm past eating, anyway."

He stood in front of the looking glass, narrowing his eyes like an artist viewing his subject.

"I hope you're managing to look a little more pleasant for our friend. The impression you make on him can be important."

She gathered her gloves and bag. "I imagine it's about the same basically as I make on you."

He turned. Reaching out, he touched her face lightly with his fingertips. "Then that'll certainly have to be changed."

She let the car roll down the incline, the jibe rankling. It was as if they were suffering from some kind of disease for which each blamed the other, seeking only the bitter and humiliating things to say. She sounded her horn vaguely, and turned onto the hill. Tires shrieked on the still-warm asphalt. The car coming fast downhill swerved violently to avoid them. Venner lowered his face into his hands. After a while he lifted it.

"If your nerves are that bad, I'd better take the wheel."

She tightened her grip, still seeing the terror on the other driver's face. Changing gear, she held the car to a steady rush. It was after nine as she cut west along the Bayswater Road. She found parking space on a side street a block south of the ice rink. Using her hand mirror, she started smoothing the fall of red-brown hair, tucking the upturned ends into place.

Venner watched her sardonically. "That's much better. Let's give him the full treatment."

She slammed the glove compartment. There was an art in biding one's time. They walked back to the lighted portico and bought spectator's tickets. The temperature inside the rink was ten degrees cooler. Beginners slithered precariously in front of a mural of snowcapped peaks. The pink walls glowed with candelabra. In the middle of the skaters the initiated leapt and spun, their faces tense and dedicated. The hiss of steel on ice made a background to the music blaring from an electric organ. She touched Venner's sleeve.

"He's over on the left — sitting alone."

The change in Venner's bearing was subtle. In that instant he became a man fearful but determined. MacLaren's table was well away from the ice over by the wall. A cool corner, avoided both by staff and onlookers. He lowered his newspaper long before they reached him. As if he'd been watching them through it, she thought. He stood, switching his brief smile from her to Venner. After the first nod of recognition, the two men lapsed into silence. The Canadian finally broke it.

"I guess there's no point in beating about the bush. Your wife says you're offering five thousand pounds to anyone ready to blow a hole in your head. Is that right?"

She looked at MacLaren sharply. He seemed perfectly sober. She had the feeling that this blunt brutality was affected for the occasion.

"Not anyone — *you*," Venner answered quietly. "And I'm not sure about the head. Otherwise the statement's reasonably accurate."

She broke in quickly. "I've told him everything, Stephen. You said there could be no half-truths."

Venner's hands were furtive in his pockets. He kept his eyes on MacLaren, his voice hesitant.

"It's not easy to talk about this sort of thing without sounding fairly bogus — especially to a stranger. But it *is* sometimes easier to die than to go on living. You probably don't believe that." His mouth shaped the beginning of a rueful smile.

MacLaren rubbed the side of his head. "I guess I've never given it much thought. Offhand I'd imagine the pressures have to be pretty strong for anyone to lose the will to survive."

"They do," said Venner. "I haven't been left the choice."

Both men seemed to be probing one another's sincerity. She turned her hands over, wondering why they chose this moment to start shaking.

"That's what I understand," said MacLaren. "I'd like to hear more."

Venner lifted his shoulders. "The subject's loaded

with the sort of emotional traps I'm trying to avoid. If
you intend to help us, I'd prefer to think that we're
rendering one another service."

MacLaren's face gave no hint of either sympathy or
suspicion.

"I'll tell you," he said finally. "It's been a long time
since I recognized society's right to tell me when a man
should live or die. I'm for hire, if that's what's worrying
you."

Venner's manner was apologetic. "I'm a lawyer and
the law's a forcing ground for platitudes. I've had to
give a great deal of time and thought to the mechanics
of my scheme. There are two factors of supreme importance, as I see things. First is to make certain that
neither of you is in danger of any kind of reprisals. The
other's that you can be certain of being paid. I can satisfy
you on both points."

MacLaren watched a skater's jump to its bungled conclusion. "I'm glad about that."

Venner brushed his hand across his mouth. "This atmosphere is hardly right for what we have to discuss. It's
impractical in any case for other reasons. There are
things I have to show you. I suggest you come back with
us to our house."

She was still unable to rid herself of a lively apprehension.

"The house might be the last place he wants to go. We
could always meet again tomorrow, Stephen."

Venner brushed aside her objection. "My wife has a
useful sense of caution. It just happens to be out of place

tonight. Our servants live fifty yards away. The house is
empty."

MacLaren's eyes were untroubled. "It suits me."

The street was sultry after the coolness of the rink. She
walked to the parked Sprite, flanked by the two men.
Venner took his place beside her. As she fished for the
ignition keys in her bag, he produced a small silver box.
He opened it unostentatiously and swallowed a couple
of white tablets. She recognized the snuffbox from her
drawing room. The tablets, she guessed, would be pure
aspirin. She touched the starting button, aware that
MacLaren had noticed her husband's gesture.

She drove fast but safely, the near-miss on the hill
still vivid in her mind. Now and again, the lights of a car
behind silhouetted the upper half of MacLaren's body.
He was sitting sideways in the narrow back seat, withdrawn from their occasional generality. She gunned the
motor at the bottom of the long incline. Halfway up, she
steered left between the looped chains protecting the
lawn. The garage flat diffused a yellow light through the
intervening shrubbery. Sound of televised gunplay
crackled through the open windows. Mrs. Collins had
switched on the coaching lamp over the front door.
Emma led the way into the house, trailing her linen coat.
When the time came for MacLaren to go, let Stephen
drive him to the station — or he could take a cab.
The thought of being left alone with him made her
uneasy. Because she was uneasy she was irritable.

She pulled the silk curtains and lit the lights in the
drawing room. The tapestry-backed chairs and deep gold

carpet, the silver jug with flowers, welcomed her home. Stephen was moving about up in his dressing room. She opened a cabinet lined with bottles. Unscrewing a thermos jar, she filled a bowl with ice.

"Make yourself a drink," she said indifferently. "If you prefer beer, there's some in the kitchen."

MacLaren was lounging deep in the sofa, looking at her portrait with half-shut eyes.

"How long ago was that done?" he asked curiously.

Her hands moved to her head automatically. "Ten years. Why?"

"You must have been a very good-looking woman." He met her full stare before breaking into a grin. "The unrehearsed boob — one of my specialities. But you know what I mean."

She beat shape into a cushion violently and left the room. Venner came to meet her at the top of the stairs. He pulled her into his bedroom and shut the door.

"Are you out of your mind?" He demanded. "Bawling your head off like that. What do you suppose he'll think?"

She rubbed the soreness in her wrists, her face hostile.

"I called — I didn't shout. Why did you bring him here, Stephen? I'd rather not have him in the house."

His eyebrows made a straight line. "Don't be hysterical, Emma. A dying man doesn't have any secrets. I want him to leave here tonight, convinced that we've bared our souls to him. And that means your soul as well."

She made a sound of disgust. "You sound like the villain in a second-rate melodrama."

"I am," he replied. "Now go back and try to act normally if you know what that means."

She clutched the door handle tightly. "Do you know the one thing wrong with this scheme, Stephen. You won't *really* be dead."

His smile was bright. "My death is one luxury you can't afford. Let's go downstairs."

They came into the drawing room together. MacLaren had balanced his tumbler on the arm of the sofa. The deep tawny color of the drink was a clue to its strength. She took the glass her husband handed her and sat down beside MacLaren. He picked up the tumbler, eying the light through it.

"You people got a hoover?"

She put her drink down as if it were lethal.

"A what?"

"A hoover," he repeated. "I'm not selling them — I just wanted to know."

Venner vanished into the kitchen. He came back lugging a vacuum cleaner. He put it down in front of MacLaren, his expression impassive. The Canadian plugged the lead in a wall socket and switched on the motor. A steady hum filled the room. He tried every door and window before resuming his seat. His manner was easy, as if the maneuver were some after-dinner diversion.

"A protective measure, that's all. Though I can't think that a tape recording would do any of us any good."

Venner's face froze on an expression of shocked disbelief.

"That suggestion is completely unjustified. Please turn the bloody thing off."

She felt MacLaren's body stiffen and relax. He tripped the switch on the hoover. The drawing room was suddenly hushed.

Venner's assumption of dignity was startlingly convincing.

"Thank you. You either accept our good faith or you don't, MacLaren. At the moment, I'm the one who's compromising himself, not you."

The Canadian rattled the ice cubes in his glass like poker dice.

"OK — OK. Old habits die hard. None of us is a candidate for Communion Class. If you're asked to kill a man, you have the right to have the odds shaded in your favor."

Venner leaned forward in his chair, speaking in measured tones.

"That's reasonable. What do you need to be sure?"

MacLaren's smile came and went quickly. "Whenever I'm sure I try not to be certain."

She rearranged her legs and spoke impatiently.

"This conversation's beginning to sound ridiculous. Why can't we have a little of this logic men are always bragging about? We're three people engaged in something from which only two can benefit." She tilted her chin at MacLaren.

Venner got up like a tired man. He disappeared into the library and returned carrying the documents she had seen in the safe earlier. He dragged his armchair nearer the sofa and drooped over them.

"I've never shown these things to anyone before — not even to you, Emma. It seemed a rather cheap play for sympathy. But since they concern us all, I'm going to ask you to look at them carefully. Dr. Davidoff is a world-wide authority on cancer of the stomach. Pay particular attention to the way he shys from guaranteeing my life from one day to another. I'm not being macabre by intention but there is more. It all speaks for itself."

She took the cardboard folder guardedly and opened it. The X-ray findings showed the middle section of a stomach. A shadowy mass like a small octopus was clearly defined. Her mouth tasted as though her tongue had touched alum. She passed the prints to MacLaren without saying anything.

Venner shook his head. "I'm sorry, old girl."

She took the letter he passed her. *Old girl!* Dear God, the lines he gave himself. The letter was written on hospital stationery and dated the previous week.

28 June 1964

Philip Pearson, M.D.
444 Harley Street,
London, W.1.

Dear Dr. Pearson,

Mr. Stephen Venner, forty-three years old, came under my care three months ago complaining of a dull, constant paraumbilical pain associated with intermittent nausea, moderate anorexia and post-prandial bloating. Physical examination revealed a well-nourished and well-developed man in no particular distress with no abnormal physical findings except for a palpable lymph node in the left axilla.

All laboratory tests were normal. Roentgenograms of the chest and colon were normal. Roentgenograms of the stomach showed mucosal folds with multiple polypoid lesions.

Gastric exfoliative material demonstrated neoplastic cells containing numerous granules of melanin. Biopsy of two nodules along the posterior gastric wall showed the presence of malignant melanoma. The primary lesion was not located.

In view of the disseminated gastric and axillary lymph node involvement, exploratory laparotomy was not considered to be necessary and the patient was discharged.

It is my opinion that the patient has approximately three months to live although his condition may begin to deteriorate rapidly at any time.

Yours,

RICHARD DAVIDOFF, M.D.

MacLaren took his time with the letter, reading it twice before handing it and the roentgenograms back to Venner. He seemed on the point of saying something and then thought better of it. Venner delved into the packet at his feet, manipulating his hands like a conjurer. He produced the acceptance slip from the Paragon Insurance Company first. He ripped off brown paper wrappings, exposing the banded stacks of five-pound notes. He pushed a couple of bundles at MacLaren.

"There's five hundred pounds there," he said quietly. "You pay your own expenses. The balance will be paid in Spain. You already know the conditions. Is there anything you want to say about them?"

MacLaren made no move to touch the money on the sofa.

"That letter's written from one doctor to another. How come you're in possession of it?"

Venner lifted his head slowly. "I stole it. If I hadn't, you wouldn't be here tonight. It's not too difficult to arrange for someone to be called out of an office — especially a doctor."

MacLaren gave the answer thought. "I'd put a match to the whole shooting gallery. Everything you've shown me. I'm not at all certain you're going to find an insurance company the easy meat you imagine. Too many people are running around who seem to know that you're suffering from an incurable disease."

"One from which I won't be dying," Venner pointed out. "And in any case it's none of your concern. Your money's already in existence. There's something else — doctors seem to take their oaths of professional secrecy more seriously than lawyers. My death will be violent enough to satisfy everyone, MacLaren."

She had a quick, reluctant admiration for her husband's performance. She was not surprised at MacLaren's sudden outburst of feeling.

"You've got a lot of guts, Venner. You owe nothing to anybody."

She watched them shake hands gravely, secretly derisive at being excluded from this expression of masculine solidarity. She was completely satisfied with the part left for her to play.

"Well, now that's settled," she said, "you might as well tell Mr. MacLaren where we're going."

"Ross," the Canadian said smoothly.

She stared at him bleakly. The unshaven tramp of yesterday, dirty and on the defensive, was almost unrecognizable. She turned her head, hearing an unfamiliar sound outside. She crossed the room swiftly and flung the french windows wide open. The shaft of light reached across the garden as far as the back wall. She ventured as far as the edge of the terrace, calling.

"Who is it — who's there?"

A cat stepped into the brightness, a tiny bell on its neck tinkling as it wreathed between her legs. She went back into the drawing room. Venner ganced at her quizzically. The floor between his chair and the sofa was spread with charts and maps. MacLaren was sitting on the carpet studying them.

Venner bent down, pointing. "This island, Santa Eulalia, is a sort of geological freak off the salt flats in the Guadiana delta. It's really no more than a few hundred acres of red sandstone planted with fig trees and umbrella pines. The house is an old coastguard station. There's no electricity and the water is stored in cisterns. That'll give you some idea of the isolated position of the island."

She shut her eyes, imagining the smell of thyme and rosemary, lizards streaking across baked whitewashed walls. The burnt grass of the tiny folded valleys would be alive with strange insects. And at night, the lights of the fishing boats would dot the darkness — the only sounds the sucking drag of the surf and a bird's strident call.

MacLaren looked up. He traced the coastline with a fingernail.

"According to this, your nearest point on the mainland is Los Gatos. What sort of communication is there between there and the island?"

"Motor dinghy," said Venner. "I've done a thorough job of research. The sea's a millpond from May to September. Anyone in a boat can cover the two miles in half an hour."

MacLaren leaned back against the sofa, his head close to her knees.

"This insurance company's bound to have an agent in the field. What do you intend doing about him?"

Venner's smile was without humor. "Let him view the body and read the death certificate. There's nothing more he *can* do. The July temperature is up in the hundreds. The local authorities require prompt burial."

MacLaren lifted his face, eyes shut. "Let me turn devil's advocate for a moment. It seems to me you're running this thing very close to the edge. Look at it this way — there are two of you on this rock in the ocean — nobody else. One finds the other dead and claims an accident. Dutch — Irish or Spanish — I know the way a cop's mind works. If you manage to disprove suicide you'll have an even tougher nut to crack — murder. And your wife will make the perfect suspect."

She sat tense with a sudden clear vision of a barred cell in a Civil Guard barracks. MacLaren's analysis of the situation was startlingly convincing — it made no difference that he would be the one to die. She waited for her husband's answer.

He gave it without hesitation. "The night before, Emma will take the dinghy to the mainland. When the time comes to go back, she won't be able to start the motor. Nor will anyone else in Los Gatos. So she spends the night on the mainland. In the morning the boat still won't start. She hires a fisherman to take her out to the island. They find me on the beach. A body with a couple of bullets in the back can't be suicide."

She walked over and poured herself another drink, unable to look at MacLaren as he put the next question.

"OK — that puts *her* in the clear. What about me?" Venner might have been reassuring a nervous client.

"You use an inflatable dinghy both to land on the island and to leave. All the other equipment will be Spanish. The bullets, the gun, the rubber boots you wear. Afterwards you sink everything you've used where there's no chance of it ever coming to the surface. I know this coastline, so does the Civil Guard. The Strait smugglers load up in Gibraltar and run their stuff ashore wherever they can. It's a ready-made solution for the police. Smugglers put in to investigate an apparently uninhabited island. I hear their boat and think it's Emma coming back. I go down to the beach and some bloody fool puts a bullet in me."

She watched from across the room as the doubt faded from MacLaren's face.

"If you'd told me all this yesterday," he said frankly, "I'd have run a mile. Suppose there isn't a moon. At a hundred yards or more you'd need a lighted target."

"You'll have one." Venner hung an unseen lantern on his arm. "I'm expecting Emma, don't forget — I'll be carrying a lamp."

MacLaren rolled over on his stomach, staring down at the maps. He measured the distance from Los Gatos to the Portuguese frontier and glanced up.

"Hey! — I hadn't realized all this was happening so close to Portugal — ten miles away, no more. I get the beginnings of an idea."

Venner answered equably. "As long as the basic requirements are met, I'm willing to leave tactics to you. Incidentally, I need a couple of pictures of you — passport size."

MacLaren got up, dusting his knees. "Unnecessary. Canadians don't need visas either for Portugal or Spain."

"The bank in Los Gatos needs them," said Venner. "For identification."

MacLaren lounged over to the windows giving onto the terrace. He stood outside for a bit, looking up at the night. A dog barked a few gardens away. He turned and came back.

"All right," he said indifferently. "I'll have them done in the morning." He crammed the two bundles of money into his pockets.

Venner rubbed his temples. "We seem to have covered everything that really matters. It's late and I'm afraid I'm tired. Emma can drive you to the station — unless you'd rather I called a cab?"

MacLaren turned away from a further study of her portrait. "I'll take the lift if it's all right with your wife."

Venner opened the hall door. "You can arrange between you where to meet tomorrow. By then, I ought to have worked out some sort of timetable. Incidentally, you'll be leaving England with Emma. There are good reasons for me traveling alone."

He came as far as the car with them. MacLaren climbed in beside her. Halfway up the hill, he spoke out of a brooding silence.

"You're a real hard case, aren't you. I don't suppose there's one in a million who'd do what he's doing. And you play the bit like a dowager duchess. What does a guy have to have to bail you out of trouble — a license or something?"

She concentrated on her driving, picking up the curves ahead in her lights. Her manner was terse.

"I've had a long training in hiding my feelings. I don't think I really have to go into it any deeper with you than that."

They swung round a bend. He hung into the safety belt, staring up at the sky.

"I guess not," he said after a while. "And it's maybe just as well."

She cut through a section of mean back streets to Kingston station. It was almost midnight. She braked in front of the booking-hall entrance and kept the motor running.

"You'd better give me a time and place for tomorrow. I'm completely at your disposal."

He unbuckled the belt. "OK. I found a flat — 246 Drayton Gardens. You might as well come there. It's the second doorbell. I'll be in all afternoon."

She sat in the parked car, long after he had loped into the station. At thirty-seven, she needed no crystal ball to know how a man was reacting to her. This one was hostile and suspicious. He was also interested. To gain the confidence he'd already given to her husband she would have to change her tactics. She lowered the top of the convertible and drove home, careless of her hair in the wind. The lights were out in the Collins flat. She made as little noise as she could with the garage doors. She took the shortcut, hurrying across the darkened garden into the drawing room. She was emptying ash-trays and fluffing out cushions when Stephen called from upstairs. The summons came on the rising inflection he affected when the hearer was in good standing.

Venner was in bed, deep in pillows, a cup of hot milk on the night table. He lifted the book in his lap, show-ing her the cover.

"*Pepys*. Listen! ' . . . my uncle's corpse in a coffin standing upon joint stools in the chimney in the hall; but it had begun to smell and so I caused it to be set forth in the yard all night, and watched by two men. My father and I lay together tonight, I greedy to see the will but did not ask to see it till tomorrow.' Do you get the picture? Both of them lying there worrying how much they've been left. And outside a couple of yokels hold-ing their noses. Hypocrisy's one of the few respectable vices."

She sat on the edge of the bed, a stranger in the one room he insisted on retaining as it had been in his mother's day. His dressing-room door was open. A cowled light shone on the automatic pistol lying on the bureau. She kicked off a shoe and flexed tired muscles.

"You didn't call me in for that, Stephen. What is it you want?"

He took off his reading glasses and looked at her.

"How was I?"

Her voice was apathetic. "Larger than life and much more impressive. Were you serious about me traveling with him?"

He rolled on his side, facing her. The book fell to the floor. "I was serious."

She picked restlessly at the bedcover. "And what about that money downstairs — is that really going to this bank you spoke about?"

He leaned back, smiling like a man remembering past pleasures. "Why not? We're going to need money and I'm certainly not hauling forty-five hundred pounds about in my pocket. The thing for you to realize, Emma, is that everything I said to him is going to happen — with the essential difference. I won't be the one who's found on the beach."

She looked at him curiously. "It doesn't occur to you, for instance, that this might be the last time we set eyes on him? That you might have made him a present of five hundred pounds?"

He pulled up his knees and leaned his chin on them. "No. With someone like you I might have been worried. But he and I have established a mutual trust. I've won over too many hostile witnesses not to recognize the signs. He believes everything *I've* told him. I wouldn't be at all sure that you made as good an impression."

The pattern was constant. First came the self-congratulation then the criticism of others.

"I wasn't meant to," she replied. "He told me on the way to the station what he thought of me. But he's very much aware that I exist, Stephen."

He dropped back in his nest of pillows, smiling.

"Then give him the occasional reminder. He might get the idea that he'd make a better job of it than I did. From his point of view, you're a very attractive proposition — in more ways than one. Excitement seems to do something for you. It's a long time since I've seen you looking more desirable."

She slid from the bed, uneasy under his flattery.

"I think I'll be able to keep Mr. MacLaren interested, Stephen, without any advice."

His light went out even before she reached her own door. She undressed swiftly, forgoing a bath for the quicker pleasure of clean linen on her bare skin. Suddenly she threw back the bedcovers. The impulse to go to the window was too strong to resist. The garden lay silent under an upturned slice of moon. The shadows by the boundary wall were deep enough to conceal the watcher her imagination created. She shivered as if a cold wind had blown over her body and dragged the curtains in front of the window. Back in bed, she covered her head with the sheets.

Ross MacLaren — Saturday 4 July 1964

H E ROLLED over, awakened by the radio blaring from the next apartment. He lay for a while, orienting himself to the unfamiliar room. Orange-colored curtains blew in the open window, matching the violence of the carpet. A short interior flight of steps led to the bathroom and kitchen unit. The partitions were made of hardboard papered with silver stars. The blond oak furniture might have come from any second-rate hotel bedroom. The overall effect was pretentious and depressing but it was a place to put your head.

He threw off the sheets. Holding on to the bed he bent his knees experimentally a couple of times. Shaved and showered, he went into the tiny kitchen. The paper sack of provisions he had bought the night before was on the table. He made tea and swallowed a couple of bananas. Throwing the skins in the sink, he wrapped himself in a bath-towel and went downstairs. The five hundred pounds Venner had given him was on the dressing table. He counted out fifty, put the ten bills in his pocket and dragged the bed away from the wall. The carpet was nailed to the floor close to the wainscoating. He levered a few nails free, lifted the underfelting and slid the remainder of the money between it and the floorboards. It was barely perceptible, distributed over an area. He replaced the nails and pushed the bed back where it belonged. He had lived too long with too little to feel easy about carrying that sort of loot around. And until it was earned it was a responsibility.

He smoked the first cigarette of the day, lying on the bed and thinking about Venner. The lawyer had given no sign of wanting pity — but then he possibly didn't rate it. Death was going to leave him beyond threat of prosecution. Had he put a bullet through his own brain, died as he lived, a lousy failure, there'd always be some broad-minded minister of the gospel ready to mumble a prayer. All the people who hadn't helped him living would make the right sounds of regret over his death. Because the essence of society's judgment lay in its hypocritical values.

He balled the damp towel and chucked it at the head of the bathroom stairs. Venner and his wife were really incidentals. It was his own behavior he was trying to rationalize. The hell with the dictionary, he thought suddenly — the words integrity and honesty were not necessarily interchangeable.

He dressed quickly, cataloguing the things he had to do. First on the list were the pictures Venner wanted. This led inevitably to the problem of his passport. It was six weeks since he had returned it to Canada House with an application for renewal. He'd heard nothing in reply. He decided he'd drop in at the government offices just as soon as he was through with the photographer. It had been a long time since he'd asked David for help. For the last three or four years he'd even been refusing the occasions traditional between them. Family birthdays, Christmas, Hogmanay. This rather than face David's carefully concealed compassion.

Ever since he could remember, David Beattie seemed always to have been somewhere in the background. The big, raw-kneed kid from the next farm over the county line — a determined second to MacLaren's first in too many things that should have mattered. It was as if David's friendship had been fixed then in a generosity that was never to weaken. A comradeship of sure values displayed in an undemonstrative Scottish style. As a consular official, it must have been still harder for Beattie to refrain from criticism.

MacLaren collected his doorkey and ran down the stairs. Choosing the sunny side of Draycott Place to walk on, he took the shortcut to Sloane Square. Girls hurried by on their way to store and office. The jibe still lingered about Englishwomen — bucktoothed bags in tweed skirts and artificial pearls — but it was completely unjustified. These kids were as cute and as fashion-conscious as you'd find anywhere. He found himself looking at their legs and using Emma Venner's as a standard. Odd to think that any one of them had probably forgotten more about sex than she had ever known. She gave the impression that she treated what was a battle as a game, always terrified that the play might extend beyond the limits she imposed.

He rode a cab to Charing Cross Road. A passport photographer's rooms perched over a store selling surgical footwear and dubious literature. The man promised the finished prints in an hour. MacLaren walked across Leicester Square and into the half-empty library. He carried an armful of Admiralty charts and maps to a corner of the Reading Room. There was no feeling of disloyalty to Venner, no intention of breaking faith. The contract was binding. But he was going in too deep to take risks that could be avoided.

The area that interested him was well charted. It extended a few miles each side of the Portuguese-Spanish frontier at the Rio Guadiana. The river at Villa Real was a quarter mile wide. No bridge was shown but there was indication of a ferry service for cars and foot passengers. Los Gatos and the island lay on the southern side of the gulf. Anyone heading for Santa Eulalia from Portuguese waters would be protected by a peninsula pointing like a finger towards Spain. Creeks crisscrossed the flat coastline surrounding Tavira. It ought to be possible to move at night from Spain to Portugal and back without being controlled. A rubber dinghy with an outboard motor would make the trip easily in those calm waters. He scribbled down a list of the things he would need. The dinghy, a light motor, fieldglasses, some sort of protective clothing. All these articles could be bought without compromising himself, in Lisbon. He returned the charts to the girl at the desk. His photographs were ready for collection. The untouched prints depicted him as staring into the camera with an expression of confident expectancy. He figured that David ought to be through with the incoming mail by now.

It was a quarter past eleven as he climbed the steps of the dirty-gray building angling Cockspur Street and Trafalgar Square. The R.C.M.P. on duty snapped a salute in answer to MacLaren's enquiry.

"Mr. Beattie — sure, he's been in an hour or more. Do you know the way up?"

"Backwards and blindfolded," MacLaren answered.

The secretary kept him waiting only seconds, flashing a smile of recognition as she opened the inner door. He walked into the office thinking that the big comfortable room somehow reflected the personality of its owner. Beattie rose from behind his desk.

"Hi, David," said MacLaren. "Long time no see."

The creases that came in Beattie's face when he smiled looked as though they were there most of the time. He had hair the color and texture of coconut fiber. His suit sagged at the pockets and his tie was the inevitable tweed tartan. He forced MacLaren into a chair, his welcome tinged with mild astonishment.

"Well, how *about* that! Liz and I were talking of you only last night."

MacLaren lifted the lid of the box of Sweet Caps.

"Not in front of my goddaughter, I hope."

Beattie's good humor was inflexible. "Why not — I shouldn't be the one to say it but Kirstie's pretty sensible. You can hardly blame her if you don't give her the chance to prove it."

MacLaren nodded and looked away. He had shared too many firsts with a toffee-haired brat for the memories to fade. The orange-peel sawdust smell of the circus; the hushed expectancy of a juvenile audience as the curtain rose on a Christmas pantomine; the thunderous rush of polo ponies, their riders' helmets bright in the sunshine.

"Suppose we don't talk about it," he said quietly.

Beattie's speculative eyes were the color of washed jeans.

"Oh sure — above all let's preserve the image — the big wheel with his pockets stuffed with movie passes and candy bars. Is this the guy you think Kirstie loves, Ross?"

"I said skip it," MacLaren said doggedly. "Do you want to hear what I have to say or do I put my tail decently between my legs and breeze?"

Beattie scraped the bowl of his pipe and stuffed it full of coarse-cut tobacco. He pushed the pile of papers out of the way so that nothing obscured his view of MacLaren's face.

"Before you start, you'd better listen to this. They had a guy on the line downstairs, a couple of days ago. Bill Eriksen switched him through to me. It was some kind of probation officer on the prowl for information."

MacLaren spread his hand. "So what — I got drunk again."

Beattie unclenched his teeth on his pipestem.

"That night, when I got home, Kirstie was waiting with a copy of the *Globe*."

MacLaren kept his eyes on a pigeon that settled on the window ledge.

"Naturally, I've always imagined the *Globe* would be required reading for fifteen-year-olds in West Hampstead."

Beattie hunched his big shoulders. "Kirstie either reads or she doesn't read. There's no censorship in the house, Ross. What she said about that piece of reporting went for all of us. 'They're bloody fools if *that's* what they think about Uncle Ross.'"

Sensing the trap, MacLaren bulled his way out of it.

"Ah, come off it, Dave! You're a good guy and all that but I've been a bum for years. It seems you're the only one who's never realized it. Listen, can you imagine what it's like to find yourself committed to a clinic for deadbeats where the help calls you 'brother'?"

Beattie was massaging his long upper lip. He spoke with quiet affection.

"But you didn't belong there — any more than you belonged on Fleet Street."

MacLaren's head snapped up. "Don't give me that old bit. We've come a long way from the crossroads store. I was a good newspaperman. I'd still be one if the hatchet men hadn't gotten to me."

Beattie knocked out the dottle and put his half-smoked pipe away in a drawer.

"I don't have to tell you whose side I'm on, Ross. But you play life the way you used to play hockey — hogging the puck. MacLaren needs no assists — he just wants to blast down center-ice on his own."

The desk phone sheared the silence that followed. Beattie said a couple of words and replaced the handset. His face wore a slightly worried expression.

"That was the Old Man. Someone must have told him you were in the building. He wants to see you."

The quickness of MacLaren's gesture sent the pigeon off in a cloud of tail feathers. Knots had tightened in his stomach.

"We've never met one another — I'd rather keep it that way. Listen, Dave. For the first time in years I've got a chance to make a little real money. Never mind how — but I need your help."

Beattie's washed-blue eyes acquired a new and watchful look. "So what do I do — stick up a bank with you?"

"See they get up off my passport," MacLaren answered. "The application for renewal has been in here for six weeks. What are they doing — waiting for Lester Pearson's OK?"

Beattie gave him a long cool stare. "That's what I was going to tell you. The Old Man blew his top when he heard of your last caper. He sent a directive down to Eriksen's office that the next time your passport came in for any reason at all, it was to be returned to Ottawa for cancellation. You were supposed to get a landing permit that saw you into Canada."

MacLaren's jawline stiffened. "The old bastard. Dave — you've got to help me. I need that passport."

Beattie opened a drawer. He slid a passport across the top of the desk.

"You've still got a few friends around. Eriksen proc-
essed your application before he officially read the directive. I've been holding it here till we had some sort
of reasonable address to send it to. Now listen. If this
thing ever comes back into the building — no matter
what the pretext — it's curtains. There's a file on you in
the Old Man's safe as long as your arm. Just about the
prize exhibit is a two-page letter from the managing
director of the *Globe*. He claims you're a helluva bad
advertisement for Canada. The record backs him up, no
matter what you or I may happen to think. Why don't
you use your head for once, Ross — there's nothing in
this country for you any more. Go on back home. I can
always find the fare."

The draft from the window stirred the papers on
the desk. MacLaren reached over and picked up his passport. He made a gesture of thanks with it. His face
muscles felt as if they had been starched.

"What else is new?" he said carefully.

"You've been part of my family for thirty-five years,"
urged Beattie. "The farm's still there. Bob and Flora
would be tickled to have you. You might even write
that book you were always talking about. Why not give
yourself a chance among real people for a change, Ross?"

MacLaren stared out of the window. A surf of sound
broke in the street below. Four thousand miles west,
the sun would be coming up over the ruffled lake, tinge-
ing the white-painted farmhouse. Out in the barn, cows
would stir restlessly as the hired help clattered milk
churns. The coffeepot would be cooking in the big bright
kitchen. Sitting in front of it, Dave's brother in his socks,

reading yesterday's baseball scores. He could even hear the long raw shriek of a Soo-bound boat in the distance.

He turned to face Beattie, reading the other's open mind. "I'm sorry, Dave," he said quietly.

Beattie took defeat good-naturedly.

"It's your life. The offer's permanent. Do I ask about this deal you're going into or not?"

MacLaren shook his head. "Not."

Beattie explored his sandy back hair. "Well, maybe it's just as well you don't see the Old Man. I've said about everything he would have done."

"A little more," answered MacLaren. He crossed the room. "A little more, Dave. I'll be back with a big cigar. Tell Liz she's still my favorite cook."

"And Kirstie?"

MacLaren was suddenly sorry for them both. "Tell her I said her language is terrible. And give her my love. So long, Dave. And thanks again."

Beattie wrapped an arm round the other man's shoulders.

"Take it easy and watch that passport like your Aunt Nelly's will and testament."

He came as far as the steps leading down to Cockspur Street. He was still there when MacLaren looked back — peering anxiously through the traffic like a man whose dog has slipped its leash.

Sun struck through the foliage of the trees on Sloane Square, dappling the shoulders of the flower seller. MacLaren bought a bunch of roses from the woman. He rounded the back of the department store and turned into Draycott Place whistling. Twenty yards from him, a black Humber cruised alongside. One of the two men leaned through the open window and beckoned. Car and MacLaren came to a halt together. The man leapt out with the snapped movements of a drill sergeant. He jerked the rear door open as his feet hit the ground. He had pale gleaming hair and an authoritative manner.

"Police officers — you're nicked!"

MacLaren's obedience was automatic. His shoulders bounced off the upholstery as the driver let in his clutch. The young cop had climbed in beside him. He wore a short-sleeved shirt and no tie, gabardine slacks and suede shoes. His eyes were flints of suspicion.

"What's your name and where do you live?"

MacLaren picked the bunch of roses from the floor. The car was being driven at speed across Sloane Avenue. He put the flowers down, searching his mind for the right formula. Long experience with plainclothes police procedure warned him to tread delicately. He answered with what he hoped sounded like confidence.

"My name's Ross MacLaren. You just about hooked me off my doorstep. What's this all about, anyway?"

The driver wrenched the Humber to the curb and cut the motor. They had stopped half a block from Chelsea Police Station. Squad cars and patrol wagons were parked at the bottom of the ramp leading to the police garage. A uniformed cop strolled by on the other side of the street. The driver waved at him vaguely.

"Bill's feet don't get any better, do they?" he said to nobody in particular.

The younger man took MacLaren's arm in a hard grip and turned him.

"Let's see what you've got in your pockets."

He ran expert fingers round the inside of the Canadian's waistband, felt the lining of his tie and inside his socks. He spread the contents of MacLaren's pockets across the seat. Money, keys, cigarettes, the two pictures and passport.

"Where'd you get this cash?" he asked brusquely.

MacLaren's eyebrows lifted. "From the bank."

The cop held up the piece of paper bearing Venner's name and address.

"Who's this?"

MacLaren rolled dry lips on a taste of tarnished metal. The distance to a cell in the building across the street had grown considerably nearer. He leaked a little belligerence into his voice.

"I'm not crazy about your manner, officer. I'm a taxpayer — not a con man."

The driver twisted in his seat to show thin hair cunningly arranged over a dead-looking forehead. His small red eyes were those of an irate boar and his nose had seen trouble.

"Taxpayer?" he repeated. "What's that? Why don't we just take him in and kick him in the balls, George?"

His partner handed MacLaren all his possessions except the passport. His eyes never left the Canadian's face.

"I don't believe you live within five miles of here. We've had you under observation for the best part of hour. Unless you can do a lot better than you're doing I'm going to run you in for loitering with intent to commit a felony. It's up to you."

The driver's exhalation sounded as if he were spitting.

"What's the matter with you, George? It's my half-day. Why don't we get this bastard inside and finish with it?"

A middle-aged woman came out of a doorway, a couple of poodles trotting behind her forlornly. Mac-Laren had to push his hands deep in his pockets to resist the urge to call her — to drag normality into a world gone crazy. He concentrated on the younger of the two cops.

"There's obviously been some sort of mistake, officer. These things can happen. I was in Canada House interviewing one of the staff half an hour ago. I live at 246 Draycott Place. Why not take me back there and check?"

He waited for the answer anxiously. There was hope just as long as he stayed out of a police station. He saw the driver's sneer in the mirror.

"I think he's gorgeous, George," the man said. "I've got a sus he's trying to compromise us."

"You're not on television," his partner said sourly. He covered his mouth with his hand, frowning at Mac-Laren. He fired the question suddenly, like a shell from an automatic weapon.

"Is there anyone at this address who could identify you?"

Even to his own ears, MacLaren's explanation was strained. "I don't know whether the manageress is in. I live alone. Surely my passport's good enough identification. Come to that — would I be offering to take you back to my flat if there was anything wrong?"

The younger cop wound up the window on MacLaren's side.

"Let's go there, Fred."

The driver stabbed life into the motor. His expression was as unrepentant as his voice.

"Certainly, sergeant. And if he turns out to be Peter Pan we're both off the Force."

He made a tight U turn in front of the police station, hooted and headed east. MacLaren was anything but relaxed. He knew enough about the way these guys operated to sense the direct danger. They hunted by sight and nose, dividing into classical roles. The blond would probably soften into the tolerant father-figure promising a lenient deal for a confession of guilt. The hardnosed character behind the wheel was the heavy, ready with the menace of violence. For these bastards it wasn't enough to *be* innocent. You still had to both look and sound innocent. He was conscious of doing neither.

The Humber slid expertly into an empty slot behind a furniture wagon. MacLaren was first up the steps, the two cops on his heels. He shut the street door quietly, glancing automatically at the hall table. There was no letter for him — no message. With luck he might be able to get these bums out of the house without any of the other tenants knowing he'd been visited by the police. He led the way into his flat.

Running lightly for one his size, the driver ascended the steps to the kitchen and bathroom. He came down again, grinning.

"Clean," he said.

He tested the springs of the unmade bed, shut all the windows and leaned against the wall like a cop in a movie. The blond straddled a chair, resting his arms on its back.

"How long have you lived here?"

MacLaren's mouth was nervous. "I moved in yesterday."

The cop against the wall grinned. "You want me to put your flowers in water?"

The man sitting down took another close look at MacLaren's passport. He tossed it on the bedside table.

"A journalist. What paper do you work for?"

MacLaren shifted his glance from one to the other and saw encouragement in neither.

"I've been out of the newspaper business for some time."

The cop lifted his chin from his forearms. "You've got over forty pounds in your pockets. What do you do for a living — come on, now, the truth!"

The driver scratched his head without disturbing the involved hair arrangement.

"Didn't you know — he's a ballet dancer, George."

He took a couple of skipping steps, crouching a little, his chin tucked into his neck. The stance tripped a signal in MacLaren's memory. He must have been out of his mind — he'd seen a hundred bums like this one shuffle over the canvas into the brilliance of arc lights. He recognized the spread nose, the thickened pads of flesh on the cheekbones, fitted a gumshield into the sneering mouth. The certainty left him bewildered.

Whoever they were, these jokers weren't cops. He did his best to preserve an expression of innocence, backing off slowly towards the door.

The blond smiled as if he read minds. He held up his left hand, opening his fingers slowly. The doorkey was concealed in his palm.

"What's your business with Emma Venner?" he asked.

MacLaren gauged the distance to the closed window. The balcony was a stepover.

"Emma Venner?" he repeated as though he'd never heard the name before.

The thin nose lifted. The blond's manner was mildly offended.

"That's right, old man, I want to know where you fit in. I've got an interest in her too. If she's a kinky bird I have to know about it."

MacLaren's quick rush took him only halfway to the window. But he had the phone in his hands before either man could stop him.

"I'll give you two minutes to get out of here," he said, breathing hard. "Then I call the law."

"Not today you won't," the blond answered, pointing at the wall. The telephone cable was cut close to the wainscoating. MacLaren's grip loosened. The phone clattered on the rest. His mind grew cunning.

"Look, if you guys are acting for her husband, I don't want any trouble, understand. I know her, sure. That's as far as it goes."

The younger man smoothed his pale hair.

"The way he lies!" He said with mock admiration. "We're not looking for trouble either — just the truth.

I might as well tell you, MacLaren, I've been on your tail since yesterday. I followed you here from the park. You haven't got a job — not a pot to piss in. Nothing but a new suit and a bagful of dirty socks. Why would anyone like Emma Venner hobnob with you?"

MacLaren's invention was rapid. "You know the way things go, surely. My luck hasn't been too good these last few months. Emma's an old friend. She's been helping me over a tough spot and nothing more. There's no law against it, is there?"

The blond man grinned like a banker about to refuse a loan.

"No law, no. But if you've any sense you'll stay away from her in future. Now open the door and let us out of this flea pit."

He held the key looped on a forefinger, swinging it. As MacLaren reached out, the blond grabbed his wrist and fell sideways, taking MacLaren to the ground with him. He rolled away as he hit the floor. MacLaren looked up. In that split second, the driver grimaced and drove his shoe hard into the Canadian's crotch. MacLaren curled into fetal position. Agony forced tears of pain past tightly shut eyelids. He heard the heavy breathing of the two men, his own keening whine. Then he was dragged upright. He hung limply, held from behind by the shoulders. His eyes were blurred slits, glimpsing a floating irridescence. A brutal weight thudded against his jaw. He spat out his bridgework, swinging his head in a desperate attempt to avoid further punishment. The same force rocked him repeatedly, staggering even

the man who was holding him. Suddenly his nervous
system refused to accept more pain. The savage beating
continued but his flesh was no longer aware of it. He
drifted high and remote into darkness. The shock of
cold water pulled him back to consciousness.

He was lying on the soaked bed, snoring through an
open mouth. Congealed blood blocked his nose. He lay
quite still, listening to the water dripping onto the carpet. Someone lifted his arms and legs, flexing them at
the joints. Knowledgeable hands prodded his ribcage
and chest. Then the smell of stale onions penetrated
MacLaren's blocked nose as the ex-pug leaned over him.

"Ah, he's all right," the voice said casually. "He's got
a couple of false teeth broken and his balls'll be sore.
You said you wanted a good job done on him, didn't
you. You got your money's worth."

The blond was repeating MacLaren's name softly and
insistently. He enforced the rhythm by slapping the
Canadian's cheeks. MacLaren opened his eyes on the
other's grin.

"This is just a warning. Next time it'll be some tear-
away with a shiv who works you over."

The word was a link with weasel-faced men sliding
from shadows etched in the night. Open razors in hand,
they sliced into living flesh for gain or revenge, evil and
sinister in a way that made a bullet from a .45 seem
friendly.

The driver turned away from the looking glass, rubbing his knuckles. His scowling ferocity had been replaced by a kind of beerhall bonhomie. He went into a

fighter's shuffle, dancing and hooking an unseen ad-
versary around the room. He pulled up, short on wind
but pleased with his performance.

"Do what he says, mate," he advised. "I seen a geezer's
nose taken off with a tool."

The blond's mouth was fastidious. "Keep your reminiscences for the billard hall. What do you say, MacLaren?"

Resentment went deeper than the beating. He had
walked into a roughhouse where everyone seemed to
have reason except him.

"Just get out of here and leave me alone," he said
dully.

The blond's face was thoughtful. "You're out of your
depth, old man. Stay away from the Venners and you'll
be all right."

MacLaren lay quite still on the bed till he heard the
street door slam below. He got to his feet, moving to
the window like a man out of splints for the first time.
He watched the Humber drive off, concealed by the
curtains. The angle was too sharp to read the number on
the license tag. But he wouldn't forget the oddly as-
sorted pair in a hurry. The younger man's voice and manner betrayed roots far from the slums that had bred
his companion.

He carried his aching body over to the dressing table.
The glass showed his face looking as if one side had been
sprayed with dark red paint. The guy had done a real
street-fighting job on him. He touched his right eye
gingerly. Fresh blood welled under pressure of his
fingers, bright and vital. A hard lump the size of a golf
ball protruded above an ear. His jaw was agonizingly

tender. He looked at his watch automatically. It was past one. He climbed the kitchen stairs rockily, the dull pain persistent in his groin. In the bathroom, he stepped out of the blood-spattered silk suit and ran the faucets. He lowered himself gratefully into steaming water. When he'd finished in the bathroom, he stood in the kitchen taking stock over a glass of scotch. His bridgework lay on the table in front of him, the two teeth snapped from the gold framework. A good dental mechanic ought to be able to fix them in a few hours. First he needed a doctor. This eye ought to serve as a reminder that his head was for thinking with. He wrapped his stained suit jacket in paper and put on an old pair of slacks. Half a dozen firms along the King's Road offered cleaning service in an hour.

Downstairs, he went back to the window and took a look at the street. Cats were dozing on sunny steps. A small boy ran by rattling a stick along the area railings. MacLaren stuffed passport, pictures and money into his trouser pockets and double-locked his flat door behind him. He waited on the landing till he was sure the hall was empty, let himself out to the street and hurried round the corner.

Thirty yards on, a small brass plate was set in the wall:

— ALEXANDER MURDOCH M.D. SURGERY HOURS 10-12.

He rang the bell, keeping his thumb on the button. The door was opened smartly by a woman wearing a surgical smock. Her expression showed the peeved resentment of a hen disturbed in laying.

"You don't have to make all that noise, you know. And anyway it's after surgery hours."

He turned slowly, pointing at his damaged eye. The sibilants whistled in his mouth.

"It's an emergency."

She backed off as he came into the hall. Then professional poise came to her aid. She gestured at the door opposite.

"Wait in there, then. I'll find out whether Doctor can see you."

A NO SMOKING sign hung over the empty fireplace. A locked bookcase held the collected works of Sir Walter Scott. There were a few pieces of terra-cotta on the mantel. Venetian blinds filtered daylight to a decent gloom. The chairs covered in shiny horsehair completed the impression of discomfort. The surgery door flew open with a blast of iodoform. The upper part of the doctor's body leaned into space — as if fixed by half a century's bending over sickbeds. Murdoch had a large bony head and a sharp nose. He spoke with a testy Glasgow accent.

"Well, come away in, man — come away in. I canna examine you from there."

The surgery fittings indicated some awareness of progress. An X-ray boom projected over a functional couch. Behind the desk was a glass case filled with sharp and probing instruments. The nurse fitted a chair behind MacLaren's kneecaps, the doctor pushed him down in it. Murdoch adjusted bifocals. His old clever fingers were as gentle as mosquitoes landing. He swabbed the damaged eyebrow clean, clucking as if he held MacLaren personally responsible for the injury. He bent nearer the Canadian's mouth, sniffing.

"And that'll be whisky you've been drinking. Aye, a fine mess you've made of yourself — it'll need stitching. How did it happen, eh? You walked into a door, no doubt?"

MacLaren winced as Murdoch explored the swelling above his ear.

"I hit myself over the head with a full bottle. Then I kicked myself in the crotch."

Murdoch felt delicately the length of MacLaren's jawline. "Open and shut — open and shut. Aye, you're a pretty sight," he said with satisfaction.

"Will you please stitch the eye, doctor. The rest I can live with." MacLaren said, looking up.

The nurse turned away hurriedly as Murdoch exploded.

"You can, can you! Well mind it well — don't come back here sniveling if you find yourself with a cracked jawbone!"

He crossed to the washbasin and rolled up his sleeves.

"Novocaine, Hetty," he said gruffly.

MacLaren grabbed at the seat as the hypodermic was inserted. He sat with closed eyes, hearing Murdoch open the instrument case. The doctor pricked the area round the Canadian's eyebrow.

"What do you feel?"

"Nothing," answered MacLaren. The flesh was completely anesthetized. He leaned his head against the nurse's stomach, conscious of the pull of the gut and the snipping of the scissors. Then Murdoch clapped him on the shoulder.

"Now see if you're not the handsome laddie!"

MacLaren stared into the glass over the washbasin. His dark eyebrow almost hid the five tiny knots. The slit was quite closed. Small globules of blood welled around the needle marks. A couple of weeks and even the scars would be hidden. He turned round.

"It's a first-class job, Doctor. Thank you."

The old man smiled. "Of course it's a first-class job. I've done hundreds of them in my time. Keep this over your eye for a few minutes. It'll stop the bleeding." He gave MacLaren a wad of impregnated cotton and sat behind his desk.

"Name?"

MacLaren invented an address to go with the alias and handed over the fee. The doctor rolled his sleeves down.

"Another blow on the same eye could be serious. I wouldn't be argy-bargying for a few days if I were you."

MacLaren made change in Sloane Square and waited to use the phone booth. Spray blew from the fountain over pigeons quarreling for crumbs thrown by old ladies. It seemed a long time since he had stopped to buy roses under the trees opposite. He stepped into the booth, moving his jaw experimentally as he waited for his number to ring.

Emma Venner — Saturday 4 July 1964

Sʜᴇ let the phone drop with a clatter and went out onto the terrace. Venner was deep in a cane chair, propped on his shoulder blades. A crimson foulard was tucked into the open neck of his sports shirt. She made so secret of her annoyance.

"Of course I've got the right number. I keep telling you — the exchange says it's out of order."

He crossed his ankles and grinned up at her.

"What do you suggest we do — pack our bags and leave the country?"

"You're not concerned — is that it?" she asked sarcastically. "The only contact we have with MacLaren and the number doesn't answer and you're not concerned."

He looked hard at her. "He left the phone off the hook — there's a bad connection — who the hell knows. Why don't you take a tranquilizer and lie down. I'm trying to work out an involved schedule."

She waited for her voice to be under control.

"I'm beginning to get tired of your pose as a master-mind, Stephen. Don't carry it too far."

He assembled the lapful of timetables and put on his reading glasses.

"All I'm trying to do is apply certain principles to human behavior— yours included and all you do . . ." His head jerked round as the phone in the drawing room rang violently. She ran inside, awkward on high heels, and lifted the receiver.

The Canadian's recital was flat, unemotional and disturbing.

"Don't hang up," she warned quickly. "Stephen's outside. I'll get him." She leaned through the open window. "It's MacLaren. He's just been attacked by two men and he wants to come here."

Venner was already on his feet and moving. She stood by his side as he put MacLaren through a rapid and thorough cross-examination.

"Go back to Draycott Place and get your things," he finished. "Then stay away from the area. In fact you'd do better to keep off the streets. Go to a cinema or something — but don't show yourself. I'll be in the Festival Gardens at half past ten tonight — that's right, Battersea Park. And listen, ring back and tell me what hotel you've moved into." He put the handset down.

She spoke stiffly. "This time I want a straight answer. He said these men kept mentioning my name. What men?"

Venner sat heavily on the sofa, knotting and unknotting his fingers.

"I should have guessed — Christ what a mess! One of

them is Annesley for sure. The description's right and he's been an actor. Coming out of jail like that, he'd know where to get hold of some sort of thug. It's all very simple after the event. Annesley started by following you and you led him to MacLaren."

She gave herself a second light. "I want to know *why* he should follow me. I'd never even heard of him till a few days ago. How could I possibly be involved with a creature like that?"

He struck himself on the forehead with the heel of his hand.

"Because I told him you were the one with the money. I ought to have known — of course he'd want to take a closer look at you. He probably followed you to the park, saw you there with MacLaren. The rest's simple. Annesley was dealing with what he thought to be a threat to his interests. Christ, what a mess!" he repeated with feeling.

She got to her feet and crossed the room and stood at the window. The sprinkler outside turned tirelessly, wetting the flowers to vivid freshness. Sun still lingered on the red brick wall beyond the sycamores. The memory hardened. She whirled round, speaking with absolute conviction.

"I *was* right last night. He was here — this man — out in the garden. Looking up at my window, long after I came back from driving MacLaren to the station."

Venner scowled across the lawn as if he expected to see latent impressions of a voyeur.

His manner was nervous. "It's possible. I don't like it, Emma. Annesley could easily get the idea that we're up to something tricky. If he ever does, we're finished."

She looked at his face, recognizing the signs of panic. This was typical behavior now that his plan seemed capable of miscarrying. But the old bitter accusations were useless. He had to be driven in a more subtle manner.

"How did MacLaren sound to you?" she asked. "He's got five hundred pounds of our money, remember?"

His eyes slid away. "I don't know. I'd have said he was more hostile than frightened."

Her mind shuffled the pieces into place. "Can you get hold of Annesley, I mean now — right away?"

He nodded slowly. "I think so. I have his home address."

"Try," she urged. "Tell him you've got to see him at four o'clock this afternoon. Don't say why — just that you must see him."

Above all, she had to keep her own anxiety hidden from Venner. She opened the door and went through to the kitchen. The large room had no more chrome or gadgets than was necessary. She had junked the old-fashioned stove years ago, ripped out a wall and put in large windows. She gave her instructions to the gray-haired woman at the sink.

"You can serve lunch in a quarter of an hour, Mrs. Collins. The cold chicken, cheese and a salad."

She collapsed suddenly, sitting down in a chair and grabbing at the edge of the table. She shook her head at the cook's clucking concern. Somehow she had to resist the indignity of fainting. She stayed in the same position till she could trust her legs.

"Don't fuss, Mrs. Collins. I'm perfectly all right."

She walked as far as the downstairs bathroom and found a lipstick. The skin round her mouth was livid against the tan. She wet her orange-slashed lips and went into the dining room.

As soon as they were alone, Venner uncapped a bottle of lager. He buried his face in the glass before he spoke.

"I got hold of Annesley. I just said that I had to see him on urgent business. He'll be at home at four this afternoon."

The weight of the heavy gold mesh on her wrist was suddenly too much to bear. She unfastened the catch and put the bracelet on the plate beside her.

"Did he sound surprised?"

Venner shook life into what was left of his beer.

"Not particularly. But that could mean anything. I told you, he used to be an actor. What's your idea, Emma? What are we going there for?"

She crumbled a piece of bread between her fingers viciously.

"To see how good an actor he really is. Has it occurred to you that we've learned something important about MacLaren?"

He wrapped a lettuce leaf around a wedge of Stilton and swallowed it. His head tilted arrogantly.

"That he wouldn't run away with the five hundred quid? I could have told you that myself."

The sooner he understood that the initiative had now passed to her, the better.

"We know that MacLaren has some false teeth. That

might well be important for identification purposes.
You'd better arrange to have them repaired immediately. Pay the bill by check — I'll see the receipt's found
with the rest of your papers."

He rubbed the back of his neck thoughtfully.

"Now you're ticking over. This split eyebrow's a com-
plication. It'll mean . . . Do you think you'll be
able to stand up to this identification?"

The way he said it conjured up a picture of a battered,
faceless body sprawled on a beach.

"Even after all this time, you know very little about
me. I'm less susceptible than you think," she said truth-
fully.

He half lifted a shoulder. "I suppose you'd have to
be — to be married to me."

She found herself remembering a force-seven gale,
without knowing why. It had swept over the sad Belgian
dunes, shaking the foundations of the flimsy hotel.
Downstairs in the bare dining room, an accordionist
played to an assembly of bored trippers caught by circumstance. She had sat at the drafty bar waiting for the
first glimpse of the cab that would bring Stephen from
the station. Gusts of wind battered the front of the
hotel, fanning sand under the doors and chasing the
reek of hot fat from the kitchen to the dining room.
Her mother was already on her fifth gin of the evening,
her eyes half shut as she acted out the monotonous tale
of self-sacrifice. Beside her, Emma had watched, taut
with the promise of escape. She'd learned the danger of
susceptibility early and well.

She pushed her plate away, no longer hungry.

"My God, how right you are."

He sat erect, his chin lifted. "The pity is that we never really understood one another, Emma."

Another woman might well have been foxed by the hand carelessly brushed through the distinguished gray hair. The sensitive mouth on the verge of emotion.

"I've always understood you, Stephen," she told him. "If you'd stood the ghost of a chance alone, you'd have walked out on me and left me penniless. This time I won't let you fail. Even if I pull the trigger myself I won't let you fail."

He dragged his chair back, his voice suddenly caustic.

"Worry about Annesley, not me — he's the one who can blow our scheme sky-high."

She looked past him to her possessions. Her body tightened. The silk rugs on the passage wall, the hammered silver tray on the hall-table. Possessions she had stalked through auction rooms and snatched from unworthy buyers.

"Do as I tell you and you can forget about Annesley. We could have saved a lot of trouble if I'd known about him in the beginning. I'm going upstairs to rest while you do some telephoning. The first thing is to get a dental mechanic. And I want to know where the keys are to the island."

He poured himself a weak brandy and soda.

"With a grocer in Los Gatos — a man named García. He's meant to supply whoever takes the house with stores. Why?"

She passed her fingers slowly over her throat. "Because I'm getting the feeling that time's becoming important. Have you done anything definite yet about the tickets?"

He carried his glass over to a chair by the phone.

"Yes. I've booked two lots of seats in the name of Mr. and Mrs. Venner. One to Seville, the other to Lisbon. Something MacLaren said gave me the idea he's going to make a point of going one way rather than the other. I played safe — I can always cancel."

She nodded, satisfied. "And how do you get down there?"

He looked up from the open phone book.

"Train to Paris, then a plane to Seville. I can't move till I get those pictures from MacLaren. It's a tight schedule but if all goes well, I'll leave tomorrow night."

She came back to the point that still worried her.

"And the rest of the money — the four thousand, five hundred pounds?"

He closed one eye. "It's already gone — via Switzerland. Payable to Stephen Venner on production of passport. His widow won't have any trouble collecting."

She left him dialing his first number and went upstairs. Behind her own door, she kicked off her shoes. The oatmeal carpet was warm underfoot, the white walls and furniture dazzling in the clear light. She drew the curtains and threw herself on the bed. Burying her head in the covers, she slept.

The ringing telephone awakened her. She lifted herself on her elbows, hearing the bedroom extension tinkle as her husband took the call downstairs. She padded into the bathroom and splashed her face with cold water. Sleep had banished her earlier nausea but the strain of the last few days was beginning to show. She made up her eyes and mouth with care and brushed her hair to burnished sleekness. This blackmailer would find she was able to give a performance as good as his own.

She rolled back the doors of the built-in clothes closet. A light came on inside. She reached past furs shrouded in plastic bags and swung out a barful of hangers. Her choice was a green shantung suit with jade buttons. She matched the outfit with a hat of Italian straw that flopped over her eyes. The last touch was the fake solitaire. It had impressed too many people over the years suddenly to have lost its magic.

Venner was in his favorite seat out on the terrace. He had changed to blue hopsack and wore a highly apprehensive look. He stood up, removing some fancied speck on his sleeve.

"I wish to God this thing with Annesley was over. You don't know him. If he gets it into his head that we're conning him — it's goodnight."

She stood for a moment, wondering how to give him back his confidence.

"Why do you let a man like Annesley hypnotize you, Stephen? What we're going to tell him is no more than he already believes — that's our strength."

He grunted. "I hope you're right — MacLaren rang again. He's moved his stuff into some hotel in Blooms-bury. He gave the impression he's going to fire a lot of questions tonight."

She pulled on her gloves. "Then we'll have to give him

the answers, won't we. Did you do anything about his teeth?"

He nodded. "I found a chap who'll work all night if necessary. You'll have to attend to it. I've left a signed check on the desk."

"How long am I likely to be away?" she asked. "I must know because of the Collinses."

"I don't know," he shrugged. "About a month, I imagine. It will look odd if you're in a desperate hurry to leave. You're supposed to weep and haunt the police offices crying for vengeance."

She looked at him narrowly. His face was ready to smile.

"What a lark," she said acidly. "Are you ready?"

Collins had washed and leathered the Sprite to summer brilliance. She bolted the top in position and tossed her hat on the back seat. Her eyes followed the route Annesley would have taken the night before, running swiftly across the lawn to stand in the shelter of the blotched sycamores. He could have taken three steps and touched her — indifferent to discovery — walking in *her* garden, sneering at her security. She had a sudden feeling of intense self-pity. She was thirty-seven years old and friendless.

Venner adjusted his dark glasses. "Are we going to sit here for the rest of the afternoon?"

She switched on the motor. His arm slid along the back of the seat. The physical contact would never quite be made. But the thought that it might would keep her bolt upright. She talked as she drove, drilling him in his part.

They left the car at the bottom of Queen's Gate and walked south. Beyond Onslow Square was a short row of modern cottages. Venner slowed, scanning the numbers. He stopped in front of a blue-painted door and lifted the knocker. A man's voice called out.

"Just turn the handle. It's not locked."

She was first into the narrow hallway. The man standing on the rope-railed staircase inspected her smilingly. Her skin contracted as if she had touched something loathsome.

Venner spoke awkwardly. "This is my wife."

Annesley seemed to test each tread for a rotting board. He closed the street door and stood with his back to it.

"I know . . . I've seen Mrs. Venner on several occasions. Won't you go through?"

He waved a hand at the room in front of them. Tired greenery trailed from earthenware pots. The floor was a welter of snarled guitar strings, sheet music and un-ironed washing. Annesley's wife had produced herself lying on her back, playing with a kitten. He kicked his way through the litter and cleared three chairs. His wife rolled to meet him, abandoning the cat and putting her head against his knee. The V of a sailor smock dipped between her breasts and she wore black stretch trousers. He pushed his fingers into her pale hair.

"This is my wife — Mrs. Venner." He turned to Venner, poker-faced. "You know one another, of course. Can I offer you something to drink?"

Emma's voice was as brittle as frozen metal.

"We haven't come here to be entertained."

"Then what *have* you come for?" asked Annesley.

Venner took his cue, speaking in a shamed, dogged tone. "I've told my wife everything, Michael."

The girl launched a barrage of laughter. It stopped abruptly as Annesley's fingers tightened in her hair. He half closed his eyes, smiling at the ground.

"No one can say you're not full of surprises. And what does Mrs. Venner think?" He lifted his eyes at her.

She looked at them both in turn.

"I don't have any illusions at all about my husband's lack of judgment. Or, for that matter, his lack of taste. They both ceased to bother me a long time ago. But what I do resent, Mr. Annesley, is the fact that you've seen fit to push your filthy way into my private life."

The girl whistled loudly and started to buff her nails. Her husband's face reddened. He flapped a hand through the cloud of smoke he blew.

"What are you trying to do, Mrs. Venner — force me into being unpleasant?"

It seemed a good moment to show her colors.

"Don't be ridiculous — nobody has to force a blackmailer into unpleasantness."

He bent down, picked up a record jacket and skated it across the room.

"I don't think I like you, Mrs. Venner," he said thoughtfully. "And I bet I know what you're going to say. You're going to say that you love him — that he's forgiven and that you'll stand by him through thick and thin. All very laudable but it won't cut any ice with the Law Society."

"For God's sake shut up!" Venner said loudly. He looked down at his shaking hands as if ashamed of the outburst. His voice was much quieter when he spoke again.

"Look at her face — don't you see that you're wasting your time, Michael. She's not interested in me. All she's interested in is the man you beat up this morning."

Mrs. Annesley suspended her care for her nails. She flicked her gaze from her husband to Venner, like a spectator at a tennis match.

Emma's laugh was short and unhelpful. "I hope that doesn't disturb your calculations, Mr. Annesley. I came here because I wanted you to understand that it isn't fear that's stopped me going to Scotland Yard. You see, I'm going to marry the man you attacked. We've both had more than our share of unhappy living. I'm determined that our life together will be free of scandal — free of the vileness that people like you bring into it. But make no mistake about this, if we're driven to it there's nothing we're not prepared to face. That includes any threat you may think you offer. What you'd better keep firmly fixed in your head is this. The only way you can get any money out of Stephen is through me. And you'll find I'm as tough as you are."

Annesley's hand came out and up, like a cop stemming traffic.

"Now wait a minute. We seem to be talking at cross-purposes. You don't want scandal. I can make it. Somebody buys silence. Whether it's you or Stevie-boy here, is a matter of indifference to me."

The light blue eyes were unswerving but she sensed hesitation behind them. She made play with the gold lighter.

"You're forgetting something. I said I didn't want scandal. I also said I'll meet it if I have to."

Annesley's lips rolled in a thin smile.

"What are you doing here then, Mrs. Venner. Buying or bragging?"

His wife knelt in front of him. "She's a liar, Michael. She's no good to any man — he said it a hundred times. She ought to be in a convent. She's lying."

Annesley sealed her mouth with his palm.

"Mrs. Venner?"

Her voice despised everyone in the room.

"I wanted to show you precisely where your interest lies. I'm leaving my husband tomorrow. We've come to an arrangement. I'm going to make a financial settlement on him in return for a divorce without scandal. How he deals with you is his own affair but you can be quite sure of this — the next move that you make to molest either Mr. MacLaren or me — I'll see you go to jail for a very long time — no matter *who* else suffers." Her glance rested on Venner for five full seconds. Then she gathered her bag from the floor and stood up.

"To be certain we understood one another, Mr. Annesley. That's why I came here. Talk it over with Stephen."

She left the room in a silence unbroken till she slammed the street door. She walked as far as her car, tore off her hat and wound down the window. She lit another cigarette, watching the driving mirror. She had a clear view of Onslow Square. A quarter hour passed before Venner appeared. He hurried by the Sprite without sign of recognition. The pointless maneuver bothered her. Annesley must know the car by sight. It was no secret that she'd come with her husband. She put the car in gear and turned the corner, Venner jumped in, twisting round and craning through the rear window.

"Get a move on. They were getting their car out as I left. I don't want them following us."

She handled the gears competently, bounced one set of amber lights and doubled back on her tracks. At Grosvenor Gardens she filtered into the eastbound traffic, circled the palace and throttled down to the park speed limit. As they neared the broad space in front of Admiralty Arch, Venner signaled her over to the curb. He wrapped his knees in his hands and grinned at her.

"Fantastic, Emma! I almost believed you myself. You left a very worried young man indeed. He's not worried about the police yet — it's the fact that you're so obviously in control of the situation. You were so impressive with all that about MacLaren and divorce that Annesley thought of another idea, a cheaper solution for you. You wouldn't make any settlement on me at all — just a straight payment of five thousand pounds to him. And he makes me give you a divorce free of scandal. You know, one might have done something with Michael. He's ruthless and intelligent."

She frowned, hearing the satisfaction in his voice. Conceit acted like a drug on him.

"And?"

His smile widened. "I can see the wheels turning. I do wish you wouldn't underestimate me. All I did was

let it filter into his head that I'd be a better proposition
with a settlement than without. He finished up with
very strict instructions. He still wants his five thousand
on the first of August but I've been told to leave you
and MacLaren severely alone in the interim. And give
your lawyers whatever they need for a divorce. He
doesn't even mind if his wife's mentioned. In fact
they're both ready to supply evidence if it's necessary."

She shook her hair back. "I feel like Joan of Arc beside people like that. I'm going home. Do you want me
to drop you?"

He turned his wrist, looking at his watch.

"No, I've got to get hold of my photographer — arrange to see him tonight after we've finished with Mac-
Laren. Pick me up in the Royal Court bar, say ten o'clock."

She switched on the ignition, the thought of Heronscourt without him a blessed relief. She'd have a tray meal
on the cool terrace as the shadows crept longer across
the lawn. And think. To deal adequately with Stephen
she needed time to think. It looked as though there
would be little time for it during the days to come.

She made the hotel bar in good time. Venner waved
cheerfully from a corner table. He stood up, greeting
her with the affectionate courtesy he used in public.
She shook her head in reply to his inquiry.

"There isn't time. They phoned from London Airport.
I have to confirm Monday's flight before midnight.
What have you decided?"

He showed her the sheaf of tickets in his hand.

"Tomorrow night. Somebody canceled a sleeper at the last minute."

She nodded impatiently. "The Collinses think we're traveling together, naturally. I'll leave with you and take a room somewhere for the night."

He signaled the waiter and paid his bill.

"As soon as I get the pictures from MacLaren I'll go on to the photographer. He's promised everything by eleven o'clock tomorrow."

"I wish we didn't have to go to this man," she said impulsively. "I know all about him being an expert, but suppose an Immigration Officer takes it into his head that you don't *look* like the picture on your passport?"

He shook his head at her. "For God's sake, Emma — let's not go over it all *again*. I know what I'm doing. With a highly skilled and professional organization behind me I'm not even taking a chance. For the tenth time — the train steward collects the passports from first-class sleeper passengers. I won't even *see* the Immigration people."

She snapped the catch on her handbag. A succession of hotel clerks, bankers and policemen had thumbed her own passport. The brief glance at the picture always seemed to be in assurance that the passport belonged to *someone*. The interest lay always in the written particulars. These were what promoted the mechanical smile that accompanied return of the document to its holder.

She gave him the look of acceptance that he expected. He was better equipped to deal with MacLaren in this mood than panic-stricken.

"I'm probably wrong," she admitted. "My nerves are beginning to show through my skin. I'll be better once we're out of England. It's been a long time since I felt as keyed up — not apprehensive, just tense."

He held the door open for her.

"Perhaps fifty thousand pounds will help you relax."

The illuminated brewery clock on the South Bank showed the half hour as they crossed Battersea Bridge. Following Venner's directions, she swung left into the park. A couple of hundred yards on, he held up his hand. She stopped the car. The remains of the Festival of Britain still lingered in the form of a few tawdry buildings devoted to carnival shows. Rifles cracked through the bawl of sideshow barkers, the shrieks from the Dodgem cars. The lakeside restaurant threw its lamplight across the water. Sad captive animals moved restlessly in forgotten corners beyond. A shoving, seething crowd of teen-agers blocked the entrance to the amusement park.

Venner craned through his window looking up at the trees overhead. A plank walk suspended in the branches made the circuit of the carnival area. MacLaren was just coming into view immediately above the car. Venner whistled softly and opened his door. He walked across to the bottom of the steps and waited for the Canadian. She watched the brief handshake, her husband's arm wrapped round the other man's shoulders. MacLaren shook his head. An arc lamp slung in the trees gave his face an olive tinge. The gap in his teeth was obvious when he smiled.

The two men settled in the car.

"Drive on," said Venner. "Under those trees by the river."

She moved the car fifty yards, off the road and onto the dirt by the stone retaining wall. She cut her lights and the motor.

Venner swiveled round, his voice poised somewhere between sympathy and apprehension.

"I don't have to tell you what a shock this business has been to us."

MacLaren sat hunched in the rear seat, a light sweater draped on his back, the arms loosely knotted across his chest.

"Uhuh," he said noncommittally. "Me, too. I'm not going to say it's the first time anyone ever worked me over. But I always figured I knew what it was in aid of. This time . . ." He shook his head and waited.

Venner managed to sound big enough to accept blame and at the same time be regretful.

"I know," he said. "I'll put my cards on the table, MacLaren. I'm entirely responsible — Emma's got nothing to do with it."

The place where they had parked was dark and peaceful. Distance diminished the noise from the amusement park. Two feet from the car radiator the river slapped ceaselessly. She watched MacLaren's expression furtively, trying to guess his thoughts. Fear on his part would be fatal to their plan. Perhaps he'd only

come to tell them he wanted no more of it. He'd open
the car door and walk away and that would be that. Her
heart shriveled at the thought.

MacLaren frowned at the cigarette between his fingers
as though surprised to find it there.

"I don't imagine you're asking me to think of a four-
letter word meaning sucker before you give me the
answer. Or are you?"

Venner's confession stayed close to the facts. He
jumped back in time to Annesley's visit to King's Bench
Walk. He was neither self-excusing nor apologetic. It
was a man's tale, told for a man. He stretched the ten-
sion taut till it snapped finally in the flat on Draycott
Place. He ended with a hint of embarrassment.

"I never imagined Annesley would go that far. And
it's obvious now that you ought to have known this at
the beginning. I'm sorry."

MacLaren's manner was puzzling. He pitched his cigarette butt through the window. There was a definite
change in his attitude from the previous night. He
seemed to avoid looking at her directly. As if the bitch
image had grown even stronger in his mind. She had
to do something to erase it.

She sat, twisting the ring on her finger. She spoke in
a low voice.

"What's the good of pretending I have nothing to do
with it, Stephen? If it weren't for me none of us would
be sitting here now." She lifted her eyes, waiting for
MacLaren to turn his head and look at her.

"I'm sorry, too," she added.

MacLaren's voice was indifferent. "Let's get off the subject. We're *all* sorry. I'd rather hear about this dental mechanic. I don't like eating steak with a spoon."

Venner was obviously relieved. "He's ready to work all night — my own dentist recommended him. One way or another we'll make this up to you, MacLaren. You've got my word for that."

The Canadian shrugged. He fished in his pocket, producing a tissue-wrapped object and a small envelope.

"The pictures you asked for. And careful with the teeth. Now that's settled, let's talk business. I want to go via Lisbon, Venner. I spent an hour this morning working at survey maps of the coastline near the frontier. I'm going to look for a place just inside Portugal — somewhere with beach frontage. If I stick an outboard motor on the dinghy, I can be on your island in a couple of hours. It's dark. Nobody sees me come, nobody sees me go."

Venner was decently short of enthusiastic.

"You're a good man, MacLaren. It all makes sense. You can buy whatever you need in Lisbon. I'll arrange for a car that you can pick up at the airport. You'll need transport and in any case you'll have a lot of gear. It's a five-hour drive down to the Algarve."

MacLaren fingered the lump over his ear. "You'd better get hold of a gun for me. An automatic for preference, large caliber."

Venner's manner lost some of its liveliness. "Why a gun?"

The Canadian sunk his chin in his palm. "Because next

time I'm jumped, I want to use it. There's another reason. They throw the key away in Spain and try you on
your deathbed. A damp cell gives me rheumatism, anyway."

"I'll see what I can do," Venner said. "But there's no
risk of that."

MacLaren's nostrils flared over a thin smile.

"Show me your crystal ball. If you can get hold of
Spanish carbines and the rest, a little old Webley Special shouldn't present any problem."

Emma broke in hurriedly. "I'll confirm our flight
tickets to Lisbon. They'll be for Monday morning.
Stephen's leaving tomorrow night. We'll have to work
out times and places where we can reach one another
by phone."

Venner considered first one toecap then the other,
brooding.

"I can only do so much. The rest is up to you two. I
wish to God there wasn't this hostility or whatever between you. It's a bad start."

MacLaren lolled back, looking at her directly.

"That's right. What *is* it between us?" he asked mock-
ingly.

She was unaccountably nervous. "Whatever it is," she
said steadily, "isn't of my making. And I could do without it. Perhaps you'll tell me what time you want me at
your hotel in the morning?"

"You just said we take off on Monday morning. Isn't
that soon enough? Or can't you keep away?" He showed
the gap in his gum deliberately, it seemed.

Venner's foot tapped caution. She made her voice

sugary. "I was thinking about your teeth. They'll be finished. I was going to bring them."

He struggled his head through his sweater.

"Call me at the Challoner any time after eleven. It's on Russell Square. And this time make sure nobody's on your tail." He turned to Venner. "I'll walk home — I need the air. If you're off tomorrow night, take it easy. And don't worry about me, old buddy. I'll be around when you need me."

She backed the car onto the hardtop. MacLaren was still in the trees when she looked into the driving mirror.

It was after midnight when they reached home. They carried their nightcaps out to the terrace. The night smelled of grass and wallflowers. The scene produced the same feeling of intense loneliness. She shut her eyes briefly, savoring the clean taste of whisky and soda.

The swing creaked under Venner's gentle pull.

"Any post-mortems?"

She spoke with a sense of foreboding — as if her answer were better left unsaid.

"He's dangerous, Stephen. Don't ask me why I say that — it's just something I feel."

He put his feet firmly on the ground, stopping the swing seat's movement.

"God Almighty — at this stage in the game! You don't feel things without reason, Emma."

She shook her head obstinately. "You asked me what I thought. I told you."

He pulled his ear thoughtfully and tried again.

"Is it that you're afraid of him?"

She was aghast at the thought. "That wasn't what I said. But even if it were true it wouldn't matter, Stephen. I don't react the same way to fear as you do."

He took the few steps to the lawn. She snapped her lighter, telling herself that she was smoking too much. The gesture had become mechanical — a screen that allowed a moment's respite from Stephen's need for constant reassurance.

He flourished his fingers in a courtroom gesture.

"He's not dangerous. To start with, nobody as dishonest with himself would be a danger. He thinks he's going to put five thousand pounds in his pocket — a bullet in me — swindle the insurance company and still manage to feel noble. He's predictable, Emma — every yard of the way. This idea he's got about a villa operates in our favor. Try to get him to let you take it for him. Point out that the less he's seen in the area, the better."

She tried to take a reef in his sail. "Have you thought about what happens if he leaves his passport in Portugal? We've no way of stopping it."

His face wore the calm confidence of a good skier at the top of a hazardous run.

"I'll simply collect it. You'll know the location of the place. It'll be night. I'll throw everything he owns in the car and drive up to Lisbon. All I have to do is get a hotel porter to phone the owner of the house — Sorry, Mr. MacLaren's been called away suddenly. I return a car hired in his name. About the same time you're discovering your husband's body I'll be in Zurich."

"I've no intention of going out to that island alone," she said in a loud sudden voice.

"Obviously not," he conceded. "You've got to produce a live husband before you can find him dead. We'll meet in Los Gatos — we'll work out the details later — pick a place where people will remember no more than the clothes I wear."

"How far do you trust MacLaren? I want to know, Stephen." She asked on impulse.

He smiled, putting a heel on the end of his cigar.

"I defended a forger once. The essence of what he said was that you could trust most men with either your money, your liberty, or your woman. The occasional sterling character could be found who could be trusted with two of the three things. But all three, never."

She snapped the terrace light off. "That's a verity I was aware of at the age of twelve. Goodnight."

Ross MacLaren — Monday 6 July —
Tuesday 7 July 1964

HE LEANED back, jamming his foot hard on the brake pedal. The cart ahead began to swing across the highway towards the cactus-bordered track on the left. The big blue Chrysler drifted close to the mule's sleek hide. Screaming tires seared rubber into the hardtop before the heavy car finally righted itself. He had a brief glimpse of the cart's occupants, somber-clad and sitting stiffly upright under an umbrella protecting them from the fierce sun. The man was fully dressed in suit and tie. The woman's head scarf was topped with a black felt hat.

He took a firmer hold on the steering wheel, doing his best to match their complete lack of emotion. A steady trickle of sweat was falling from his armpits onto his ribs. Five hours of this kind of thing had left him nervous and irritable.

"Just one more like that," he promised, "and I'll be a cot case."

Emma's dark glasses were covered with a film of dust — her oatmeal-colored dress stained and creased from the journey. But she still retained her imperturbability. Ever since they had landed in Portugal her manner had become increasingly friendly. Her cool patience had carried them through the subtropical glare of downtown Lisbon. Using a café opposite the ferry terminal as headquarters, she located the stores selling the equipment on his list. She offered neither criticism nor approval of his plans. She watched his face constantly, chain-smoking and pushing the hair from her eyes. He knew for certain he was being given the business but had no idea why.

She answered casually. "They've probably been doing that in exactly the same way for thirty years. You missed him. That would be enough, from their point of view."

"Then they're crazy," he said obstinately. "They use the highway like we used to use Old Jack Fogarty's river-bottom. Dogs, goats and sheep, lying all over the place. Even the kids don't seem to want to grow up and have troubles."

She laughed and then sat up, pointing ahead. "Look — doesn't this make you feel better?"

The monotony of close-coupled hills covered with arbutus trees, indefinitely repeated, was gone. Dazzling white houses dotted slopes where fig trees like fat spiders crouched over the rich red earth. Smoke from a tug in Lagos harbor plumed the translucent air. The wind blowing through the ventilators smelled strongly of thyme. He changed gear, forking left at the bottom of the hill. She map-read accurately, giving him plenty of time to respond to her directions. They took the bridge over the estuary, leaving behind the ugliness of the fish canneries. Now the highway ran roughly parallel to the coastline. Once out of the belt of alluvial rice fields, they were back in the lee of the hills. The roofs on the roughcast farmhouses dipped like pagodas, with white, fretted chimneys. Geraniums grew like weeds on each side of the road. The arroyos were ablaze with oleanders and surrounded by groves of olives, almonds and caribs. Beyond Portimão, whitewashed walls along the route protected the wax-leaved orange trees. It was past six but every four-legged thing had crept into the shade, avoiding the hot hand of the sun.

His fingers drummed the steering wheel nervously.

"We can't just keep driving. Otherwise we're going to finish up sleeping on the beach."

She leaned forward, lifting her hair from the nape of her neck so that the breeze blew on her skin.

"I thought you were making for Tavira."

"I just changed my mind," he said briefly. "We'll try Santa Cruz. There's bound to be a place to eat and you can do your telephoning from there."

Venner's unsigned cable had been handed to her at Lisbon airport. It was datelined Paris, at eight o'clock that morning: ALL WELL STOP TAKING PLANE SEVILLE FOURTEEN HOURS STOP TELEPHONE ALFONSO THIRTEEN TONIGHT.

He swung the Chrysler onto the cutoff. The metaled road snaked down the valley for a couple of miles and then dropped sharply. The way into town was along a street of flat-roofed houses washed in primary colors. It ended in a square where there was water, flowers and stone benches. He stopped the car in front of the service station and took his bearings. A few women were still peddling fruit and vegetables in the open-air market. Many of the parked cars bore British and German registrations. The invasion from the north was evident. Foreign-language newspapers were on sale outside the store at the bottom of the steep hill.

A bar thrust its terrace over the market. A canvas awning shielded the half-dozen tables. A sign outside offered prawns and lobsters for sale in four languages.

MacLaren stuffed his money and passport into a trouser pocket and nodded at the terrace.

"Let's try this joint. At least we'll be able to get some of this filth off."

She peered into her hand mirror, wrinkling her nose at what she saw.

"Anywhere with running water suits me."

He locked the car, walked round the back and tried the trunk. Barefooted fishermen sitting on the benches watched the performance blankly — as if its purpose were utterly beyond their understanding. The bar was spotless, the lavatories civilized. He came out to find Emma already sitting at a table. A thin waiter in a white jacket with gold epaulettes held a sheaf of menus against his chest. He ran the three words into one.

"English-Deutsch-Français?"

"English," MacLaren said.

The waiter whipped out a menu with a cardsharper's dexterity. The dishes were numbered to avoid any confusion. MacLaren ordered, his hand describing an outsize glass.

"And beer — *cold* beer."

The meal was perfect — the salt freshness of jumbo prawns defying the tang of sparkling lager. MacLaren wiped his mouth, the knot in his stomach unraveled. He lit a cigarette, releasing the first inhalation with satisfaction.

"This place is near enough to the frontier and it gives me the right feel. I might even ask this guy if he knows anything about a house for rent."

He watched her reaction speculatively. His first intimation that he'd look for a house himself had obviously disturbed her. Her objection made no sense. The whole point of holing up in Portugal was to fix an alibi. To do that, the more he was seen in the area, the better.

She glanced at her watch. "Isn't it a bit late for that? I thought the reason for coming here was to make sure we had a place to sleep."

He nodded. "It still is. We might be able to combine the two things."

Her eyes held steady then she shrugged. "Do whatever you think best."

He called the waiter over. "Are there any hotels here?"

The man's shoulders lifted. He broke into rapid Portuguese.

"Excuse me but I do not understand what the señor said."

MacLaren let him go. "That one doesn't even get us on first base."

He looked across at the neighboring table, aware of the scrutiny of the couple sitting at the top of the steps. They had the air of personal ownership that said permanent residents.

MacLaren smiled. "You don't happen to speak English, do you?"

Sun had leathered the long foxy face, faded the military mustache. The man's body had been dehydrated to an angular framework hung with white drill.

"I believe so," he said in a pukka sahib accent.

MacLaren gestured apology. "Then perhaps you could help us. We just got in. What's the hotel situation like here?"

The woman neighed like an overwrought mare, black eyes snapping in a ravaged face. Her clothes looked as though they had been assembled by pure chance.

"You must be mad — coming to Santa Cruz in July and asking about hotels."

MacLaren felt the flush creeping up his neck.

"Just tired, ma'am."

The man stuffed his newspaper into a jacket pocket and left a couple of coins on the table.

"Come, Lorna," he said quietly. He stood up. "There is one hotel in Santa Cruz," he observed clearly. "Three *pensions* and, I believe, some two hundred furnished rooms. I'm quite certain you haven't a chance of getting in any one of them. And no one here ever heard of a Diner's Card."

He took the woman's elbow and guided her down the
steps. They walked away up the hill, looking neither left
nor right.

MacLaren watched them out of sight, completely puzzled.

"Now what in hell was all that about?" he asked.

Emma's quick smile held a hint of malice.

"We didn't ask permission to come here — they resent it. He looks as if he's spent his life having the na-
tives flogged. But we've completely made their day, quite
obviously."

He looked over the parapet at the crowd returning
from the beach. It was noisily Portuguese and colorful.
Across the square, a guitar was playing *fados* in a cellar
bar.

"I guess we'd better move," he said after a while.
"We'll try the next town."

He was halfway to his feet when a voice hailed him
in English. A stout man in his late fifties was steering his
way through the tables, scattering the chairs in his haste.
He had one arm lifted in a sort of apostolic blessing. A
cane dangled in the crook of the other. He wore volu-
minous shorts and a faded bush shirt. He bowed gal-
lantly to Emma and thrust a visiting card into Mac-
Laren's hand. It was gilt-edged and beautifully engraved.

    Baron Casimir Reidemeister
    Romanian Foreign Ministry

(*Ancien régime*) had been rubberstamped across one
corner. The Baron had a grave plump face, a full mouth
and Tartar eye. He flipped a chair under his large rump

and sat with both hands on the table. He spoke English with command and an exaggerated enunciation.

"You must excuse this intrusion but I couldn't help overhearing your inquiry. As the oldest foreign resident in Santa Cruz, I must take it as a duty to apologize for Colonel Lubbock. His rudeness is characteristic. He has an intense dislike of Americans, I'm afraid."

MacLaren tilted his head. "Is that right?"

The Baron warmed. "But perhaps you're English and not American. In former times, some of my oldest and dearest friends were English. That regrettable war made havoc of so much. You were inquiring about hotels — how long were you thinking of staying here in Santa Cruz?"

The waiter's interest in the table had grown with the Baron's arrival.

"I don't think we'd decided," MacLaren said casually. "Is there any good reason why you ought to know?"

The Baron assailed the black stubble on his scalp vigorously.

"I am aware that we live in a world of crumbling social values but surely a gentleman may still render service to another?"

MacLaren slid his chair back a few inches. Emma had become completely silent but her eyes signaled caution. He was less impressed. The fat stranger's approach and manner were too obviously harnessed to some mild form of confidence trick. Meanwhile the terrace was cool and his stomach content.

"What exactly did you have in mind?" he asked curiously.

The Baron's stare was orientally impassive. "Merely to be of assistance to you and your charming wife." He bowed again to Emma, this time touching his heart.

"The lady isn't my wife," MacLaren said bluntly.

The Baron's wave was expansive. "References without meaning, sir. Entirely without meaning. May I offer you something to drink?"

MacLaren shrugged. "Emma?"

She lifted a hand fractionally. "It's almost seven. We still haven't found beds for the night."

The Baron looked round the bar quickly before leaning forward and drawing them into his confidence.

"I have a small house in the country — about four kilometers out of town. There is a quiet beach of great beauty. A perfect setting for people who wish to be alone. I assume you have a car?"

MacLaren nodded. "The blue Chrysler parked across the square. Do you mean this house is for rent?" he asked attentively. The Baron's fulsome nonsense suddenly took on point.

Reidemeister showed strong white teeth. "In former times I should have been glad to offer you my hospitality. Alas, my circumstances are reduced. I am obliged to let the villa to people I find — shall we say — sympathetic?" His smile hinted at some secret knowledge.

MacLaren dealt with the implication firmly.

"I'd better explain, Baron. This lady is traveling on to Spain in the morning. I'm the one who's come to the Algarve for peace and quiet. I'm interested. Could we have a look at your house?"

The Baron hissed loudly. The waiter buttoned his tunic and skipped across the terrace.

"This gentleman's bill," Reidemeister said imperiously. He overruled MacLaren's objection and was first down the steps. His squat body rolling slightly, he prodded his way through groups of children, using the end of his cane as a goad. Once in the back of the car, he sat contentedly munching a clove of garlic.

The narrow road climbed past a fig-drying plant until the whitewashed cottages scattered into the far distance. Suddenly he leaned over the seat, his breath violent.

"To the right now — and you must go carefully."

The dirt track cut through an almond grove. There was barely enough room to maneuver the Chrysler between banks menacing with spiked cactus. Fine soft dirt rose in clouds as the heavy car lurched in and out of the potholes. After a quarter mile, the track ended abruptly. The red roof of a single-story villa showed over the enclosing wall. Eucalyptus trees screened the house from east and west. Bermuda grass grew in thick patches on the sandy slope down to the beach.

The Baron unfastened a pair of rusting iron gates. He stood aside for them to enter, sniffing the air appreciatively. The small sheltered garden was overrun. Tangled carnations encroached on unpruned rosebushes. Tomatoes and melons grew wild in the shade of canna lilies. The mauve mass of creeper was murmurous with bees. Reidemeister pushed open the front door, stepping back smartly to avoid the shower of falling earwigs. He stamped them into the ground methodically.

"Repulsive creatures but quite harmless. There are no scorpions, thank goodness. At least I've never seen one."

He bustled through the rooms, opening doors and shutters till the final horror was exposed. The three bedrooms had concrete emplacements for the mattresses.

"Very hygienic," explained the Baron.

The curtains were uniform throughout the house. Fly-spotted muslin ringed to bamboo poles. There was a preponderance of cheap scratched furniture and plastic figurines. The Baron ushered them into the kitchen, tapping inventory with his cane.

"A fine refrigerator. In former times they made them to last — not like this modern rubbish. And look!"

He turned a faucet. The rusty dribble gathered momentum. It was some time before the flow covered the bottom of the sink.

"Fresh water," Reidemeister said gratuitously.

MacLaren pushed his head into the bathroom. What appeared to be a lifetime's supply of used razor blades made the window ledge lethal. Three large spiders lurked in the tub. He went back to the sitting room. A small door cut in the white wall gave access to a path leading down the slope. At the end was a crescent-shaped beach a couple of hundred yards long. High pine-topped bluffs formed the horns of the crescent. Emma stood beside him, looking down at the sea slapping the tawny sand.

"Why don't you take it?" she said with quiet urgency.

The Baron trod delicately into the room. He sagged in

the discomfort of a cane armchair, staring gloomily into the empty fireplace.

"An ideal setting for anyone who needs peace. May I ask your profession, sir?"

MacLaren pulled the window open, dislodging a shower of dead flies. The air smelled of the surrounding pine trees. A mile or so out to sea, a sailing boat was tacking into the setting sun. Everything about the place was right — its seclusion — the perfect approach to the beach. In that calm water the added distance would mean little. The outsize tank and spare drum of fuel would take care of the extra kilometers between there and the island.

"I'm a journalist," he said casually. "What sort of rent are you asking?"

Reidemeister leaned his chin on his cane. The light bulb glowed brighter as if on cue. His cane lifted slowly, indicating a telephone half hidden under a pile of old magazines.

"You have every modern comfort. The house is usually let to Count and Countess Mayenfels, two of my oldest and dearest friends. They take it for the entire summer. A family bereavement prevented them from coming this year. Shall we say thirty pounds?"

MacLaren tucked his shirt into his trousers. "A month?"

The Baron chuckled appreciation of the joke. "A week. With light and telephone extra."

MacLaren threw the window wider and crossed the room. Reidemeister's eyes brightened at the size of the roll the Canadian produced. MacLaren put twenty five-pound notes on the table.

"I'll give you a hundred pounds till the first of August. You pay the extras."

Nimble fingers swept the money into the Baron's wallet.

"Done," he said quickly. "We are gentlemen. There is no need for an agreement. I am happy to confide my possessions to your care." He waved a plump hand round the room, dwelling on a highly colored lithograph of an improbable waterfall.

A bamboo shelter inside the garden walls served as garage. Reidemeister helped carry their bags into the sitting room. His face was dangerously red from the unaccustomed exertion. He dropped the heavy suitcase with relief.

"Heavy. It might almost be gold!" He puffed his cheeks to show that he was jesting. "Sheets and blankets we must fetch from town. How many beds will you be using?"

Emma stood in the doorway, a piece of the clothing she was unpacking trailing from her grasp.

"Did I hear you say how *many?*" she asked cuttingly.

"Skip it, Emma," MacLaren said quickly. "OK. I'll come in and collect whatever's necessary. I can pick up a few stores at the same time."

She turned abruptly on her heel. The bedroom door slammed. The Baron's stocky shoulders lifted.

"Patience," he advised. "With a woman of this temperament it is necessary. That hair, those eyes — a creature of fire and brilliance."

MacLaren picked the car keys from the table.

"She's my aunt. Let's go!"

They parked on the town square again. The Baron led the way to the bottom of the hill. Every table on the terrace was occupied. The Lubbocks were back, strategically placed so that they commanded an all-round view of the scene. The Colonel glassily ignored Reidemeister's polite salutation. His wife's observation, delivered in a penetrating voice, turned every head in the bar.

"There's your answer, Charles. Not that it was unexpected!"

The Baron waddled past, unmoved. "The woman is barren," he said, "and the Colonel's rank purely temporary."

The steep hill ahead was thronged with tourists inspecting the contents of store windows with marked suspicion. The women had changed to the inevitable floral-patterned dresses, the men to nylon shirts. They talked to one another across the street to the accompaniment of high, nervous laughter. The Baron moved forward, his cane carried at the charge. At the top of the hill, he paused for breath, pointing into the corner store. Sausages and hams hung from the ceiling of the ill-lit interior.

"I advise you to shop here. If you mention my name they will give you a discount."

Countless steps connected the two town levels. Reidemeister turned left into a quiet tiny square. In the center was a church topped by a gilded belfry. Bougainvillaea clambered over the end house, paling the colors of the tiles set in its facing. Pigeons perched on the stone parapet that sealed the sixty-foot drop to the rocks below. A bell sounded in the church tower, tolling the hour with aloof clarity. The hubbub of the town below was remote. Reidemeister pushed open a heavy-timbered door. The stone floor was covered with fine straw mats. A seventeenth century breastplate was ruddy in the last sunlight. He opened a second door. The outer wall of the room was an extension of the cliff face. In front of the enormous window stood a telescope on a tripod. A motto was carved over the granite fireplace: QUANTI EST SAPERE.

A tiny Madonna smiled from an ikon. There was a prie-Dieu, its wood blackened by age. The carpet consisted of a dozen or so sheepskin rugs stitched together. Other than the ikon, there was a complete absence of painting or ornament.

The Baron clapped his hands sharply. An Arab girl in her teens slid into the room on bare henna-dyed feet. She wore Turkish trousers fastened at the ankles with silver clasps, a bodice covered with metal-thread embroidery. Her coarse black hair was tied in a chignon. The tattoo markings under her lower lip added to the strangeness of her smile.

"This is Fatima," said the Baron fondly. "My ward and my housekeeper. Fatima speaks English, French, Arabic and Portuguese. All of them fluently."

MacLaren nodded at the girl uncertainly, the transition in the Baron's mood and surroundings for the moment beyond him. Reidemeister continued to catalogue the girl's accomplishments — much as the owner of a well-schooled horse might have done in its presence.

"Fatima also dances and plays the nose flute. But her cooking, alas . . ." He shook his head, continuing to smile at her benignly. "Sheets and blankets for two beds at the villa, my lamb. And glasses and ice."

She came from the back of the house, carrying a copper tray. She put it on the low table by Reidemeister together with a bottle of whisky. He flicked his hand at her. She touched her own to her heart, her lips and forehead and left the room as unobstrusively as she had entered.

The Baron tipped after her like a ballet dancer. The vein in his neck bulged with the effort of concentration. He turned the door handle slowly with breathless patience. He flung the door wide with a sudden dramatic gesture. The girl's laugh echoed in the empty hall — a dog barked. Reidemeister's expression was completely unperturbed. He resumed his seat and poured scotch into a couple of tumblers.

"Ice and soda," he said easily. "Now tell me — what brings you to Santa Cruz?"

The sun's last dazzle was extinguished on the horizon. MacLaren touched the barrel of the telescope idly, turning it towards the coastline to the east. A humped bluff hid the crescent-shaped bay and the villa above it. He gave himself a little more soda, a small hammer beating at his temple.

"I'm not sure whether I know the right answer to that one. You mean you don't like what I've told you already?"

Reidemeister's foot kept up an incessant drumming.

"I hope you won't take offense. Remember I've been in Portugal for twenty years. It's interest, not curiosity."

MacLaren looked through the front window into the square. The pigeons were wheeling and swooping over sparrows taking a dirt bath. The innocence of the scene, the Baron's bland voice, seemed carefully designed to suspend any critical faculty.

Reidemeister's clasped hands and tolerant smile gave him the air of a Jesuit confessor.

"Come," he urged, "be reasonable. Are you writing a book?"

MacLaren shook his head. "I told you — I came down to the Algarve for peace and quiet."

The Baron's gaze was knowledgeable. "A contemplative period, perhaps. In former times I used to be an omnivorous — is that the word? — reader. What is your particular subject — politics?"

MacLaren touched his eyebrow self-consciously. The new teeth fitted as well as the originals — he wasn't lisping. Yet something about his appearance seemed to fascinate the Baron.

"I'm one of those odd people who can't understand politics," he answered. "I write about crime. It's not unlike politics — the same cast with a little more action."

The Baron's brow creased. "A somewhat jaundiced observation. Do you fish?"

"I don't have the temperament."

"Then perhaps you're interested in land?" the Baron asked softly.

An admission would have the advantage of coinciding with Reidemeister's inspiration. Failing that, the cross-examination looked like going on all night.

"I might well be," said MacLaren. "If I could find some at the right sort of price."

The Baron's smile was content. "Experience gives one the feel, you know. I am seldom wrong. In Santa Cruz?"

MacLaren held his glass to the light. "Twenty kilometers in either direction. I still meant what I said about peace and quiet. I've just been involved in an automobile accident."

Reidemeister glanced at his watch. "I told you when we first met that I found you sympathetic. Come!"

He beckoned MacLaren to the open window and swung the telescope so that it trained on a large concrete building a hundred yards or so distant. He adjusted the focal length of the powerful lens and straightened up, his voice a little husky.

"The end room — the one with the red towel hanging on the balcony."

MacLarent bent at the eyepiece. The apparatus brought the naked girl embarrassingly near. Concealed from any normal form of curiosity, she was sitting on her bed buffing her nails.

The Baron swung the telescope seaward again. He made little fluttering movements with his soft womanish hands.

"The Lubbocks' niece. Antonia Rillington-Barker. She does me the kindness of taking her bath every day at this time. Unmarried and unattached. She will be spending the winter here. What did you say your name was?"

"Ross MacLaren." There was humor mixed with the parade of middle-aged lechery. "I guess I'll be getting on back," he suggested.

The Baron made a gesture of dissent. "First listen to what I have to say, Mr. MacLaren. I'm afraid I was over-enthusiastic in my talk about the villa. I know its real worth, of course. But one has three months only in which to meet the very large outgoings. I must warn you that the foreign colony here spends most of the time in-venting scandalous stories about me. Success breeds envy. And I am a successful man. Any land that is worth buying in this area is already under my control. I shall be happy to place myself entirely at your disposal, Mr. MacLaren. Five per cent covers my honorarium. That includes the necessary formalities with the Camara — our City Hall. The President is one of my oldest and dearest friends."

He looked at the melting ice in his glass. MacLaren got up.

"That sounds reasonable enough. I'll look you up in a few days. I'll be glad if you keep this conversation to yourself in the meantime."

The Baron trapped a fly about to explore his baggy shorts.

"We must have dinner together soon. We might even invite Miss Rillington-Barker." He heaved himself to his feet and opened the hall door. A pile of sheets and blankets had been left on the chest outside. He piled them onto MacLaren's outstretched arms.

"You'll find that with me most things are possible."
He laid his finger along his nose and winked.

"That's very useful," replied MacLaren. "Goodnight."

He crossed the square, already deep in violet shadow.
The corner store was still open. Reidemeister's name
promoted heel-clicking alacrity in the proprietor. A
small boy carried the bed linen and provisions down to
the parked car. The way out was made hazardous with
unlighted mule carts and laden burros. A team of oxen
plodded out of the dirt track leading to the villa. Mac-
Laren pulled the Chrysler over on the shoulder of the
highway. The man herding the oxen lifted his hat, his
salutation incomprehensible. The passage of the Chrysler along the lane set every dog in the neighborhood
going. Canine clamor followed him as far as the house.
He drove through the gates and locked them behind
him. Lights shone through the curtained windows. He
dropped the food and bed linen on the kitchen table and
called Emma's name. She answered from the sitting
room. The floor had been swept spotless. She had made a
serviceable lampshade out of a straw basket. Her hair
was screwed back and tied. Without any makeup at all
her face was oddly unfamiliar — that of a younger sister
masquerading in her place. She had changed to a fisherman's shirt over dark blue slacks.

"I'm sorry if I was gone long," he offered.

Her face was stiff and aloof. "An hour and a half."

He found the stricture unreasonable. "You ought to
have said you'd be lonely. I'd have hurried on back."

"I haven't *said* I was lonely," she persisted obstinately.

He balled his shoulders. "Then you've got nothing to beef about. The Baron kept me. A charming character and no fool."

"He looks like a toad," she said shortly. "I hate that sort of old lecher."

"For all we know he teaches Sunday school," he said lightly. "He seems to have made up his mind that I'm here to buy land — that's what I *think* he thinks."

She walked out. He heard her making up the beds. After a while she called from the kitchen.

"Do you want to eat again or shall I put this food you bought in the refrigerator?"

"Just bring the wine bottle," he answered.

She carried in the wicker-covered carafe and one glass. She watched him pour the rough, red wine. He shut his eyes and spoke his mind.

"For Crissakes stop acting like a convent girl at a truck-drivers' convention. You're not going to be raped — not even kissed. In fact I'd as soon lock my door as have you lock yours. Do you understand that?"

Her smile was gently ironical. "I could hardly avoid it, could I. Whatever you feel about me, I'm neither mistrustful nor afraid of you. It's just — I don't know — after seventeen years of being told you're abnormal I suppose you begin to believe it."

He pulled the curtains back. The gas flares of the first fishing boats bobbed out in the darkness. He picked up the phone.

"Let's try to put that call through."

It took five minutes of bad French and a willing operator to book the Seville number. The response came with surprising speed. As soon as he heard Venner's voice he handed the receiver to Emma. It was a while before she hung up.

"How much of that did you hear?"

"Very little," he said. "What's the score?"

"He's got everything that's necessary, he told me to tell you. I'm meeting him in Los Gatos tomorrow evening. He wants you to make a trial run tomorrow. I'm to phone back if for any reason it's impossible."

The idea made sense. A preliminary trip would break in the outboard motor — allow him to fix up a system of navigational bearings. He looked out through the window. The beach was a pale half hoop against the darkness that merged with the sea. Another week had to pass before the moon waxed large enough to be dangerous. Right now, night visibility at sea was down to a couple of hundred yards. The real snag was the added distance from Santa Cruz to the island. The run would take at least six hours. The timetable he'd worked out allowed him an hour to fulfill his contract, getting him off the island and back into Portuguese waters before dawn broke. He was going to sink the dinghy deep enough to make discovery impossible and swim ashore to a cache of dry clothes. The spot he'd located was a mile or so outside Tavira within walking distance of the bus terminal. In summertime, there'd be nothing strange about a foreigner boarding the Santa Cruz bus at seven in the morning.

"It doesn't get dark before ten," he objected. "This means making the trip back in broad daylight."

"No, it doesn't," she corrected. "You can stay on the

island all day. Nobody will see you from the mainland.
You make the return journey as soon as the light goes."

A nightjar was raucous out in the pines. She sighed
deeply. He put the question to her point-blank.

"What is it you're holding out on me? There's something making my toes curl — and I don't like it."

She looked vaguely resentful. "I don't suppose you're
superstitious?"

He lifted a puzzled face. "I don't blind people at the
next table throwing salt over my shoulder — and whether
or not I walk under a ladder depends on what's happening overhead. What exactly did you have in mind?"

She looked at him, her green eyes steady. "The few
good things that have come into my life have been by
accident. The moment I've started to analyze them, they
seem to have gone as quickly as they came. That's what I
mean by being superstitious."

She was trying very hard. The lips parted, the eyes
wide and clear. But his toes still curled.

"I'm not dead-certain that we're talking about the
same thing," he replied. "But I'd just as soon make a
play for a boa constrictor. I'm going to take a look at the
beach. You do what you like."

She shifted on the battered sofa. "You've just proved
my point. I'll try to remember that you're on nobody's
side but your own."

He opened the door. "Isn't *everybody?*" he asked and
walked out into the garden.

He slithered down the slope, ankle-deep in loose sand.
High tide had left a ring of driftwood and tar globules.
The beach was still warm to his bare feet. He looked back

at the house. Her shadow moved across the sitting-room window. Silence ringed the villa. The branches of the eucalyptus trees shivered in the breeze. He pulled up his trousers as high as he could and stepped into the water. The surf rolled gently, unbroken by submerged rocks. It lapped his thighs, faintly phosphorescent. He could inflate the dinghy and row out unobserved. Once he was near the fishing fields, the sound of the outboard motor would be lost in the noise of heavier vessels. He waded back to the beach and wrung the water from his soaked trousers.

She was still sitting on the sofa. She looked up, her voice carefully impersonal.

"I want you to know that I don't make the same mistake twice. That's all."

He stretched lazily. "It's a good rule. Conditions down there are perfect. I'll make the run tomorrow."

She passed her hand over her hair. "I don't know whether I mentioned it — Stephen said to bring your passport. Something to do with the bank and your money."

"That can wait," he said decisively. "If he wants me under wraps on the island, I won't be going near any bank. My passport stays right here where it's safe till the time comes."

She seemed reluctant to pursue the point. "That's what he probably meant. He was speaking so quickly that I lost some of it."

He sat on the edge of his bed till she was finished in the bathroom. He heard her mules slap past his room, her door close. A few copper-colored hairs clung to the edge of the washbasin. There was a pot of face cream on the shelf. He brushed his teeth and put out the lights. Like an iceberg, there was a lot more to Mrs. Venner than showed above the surface.

He finished his shave leisurely and walked into the sitting room. The morning had broken fine and clear, the sea unruffled under a sky without cloud. At a quarter to ten the beach below the villa already shimmered under a heat haze. Emma was still in the kitchen washing up the breakfast things. She answered his summons, rubbing some sort of lotion on her hands. She wore a short-sleeved dress of Madras cotton, the pistachio-green a shade less striking than the color of her eyes. She had been first up, aloof and uncommunicative. Her packed bags were already in the car, the sheets and blankets she had used stacked neatly at the foot of her bed.

"As soon as I get my stuff out of the car we'll be on our way," he said.

She stood in front of the looking glass, wielding an eyebrow pencil. Turning her head she answered, "Whenever you say."

The submissiveness of her tone was probably meant to disarm him. He pitched a cigarette into the fireplace.

"OK. Give me a hand."

He unlocked the big car trunk and gave her his watch. "Time me — *now!*"

The dinghy was stowed in a kitbag. He worked swiftly, unpacking and laying the rubber-proofed shell on the grass. He fitted the nozzle of the CO_2 cylinder in the main buoyancy valves. The craft inflated quickly. He repeated the process with the thwart and secured the toggles in the floor patches. It took only seconds to ship the outboard brackets to the stern. He wiped the sweat out of his eyes.

"How long?"

She gave him back his watch. "Eight minutes, thirty-three seconds."

He nodded to himself, satisfied. The dinghy was ready for the water. It could carry a full-grown man and three hundred and fifty pounds and stay within the safety factor. He lifted out the small power unit. The single-cylinder motor had fixed drive and a four-bladed propeller. It weighed slightly more than the dinghy, around thirty pounds. A spare drum of fuel, jointed oars and a frogman's suit completed his equipment. Underneath the suit he'd wear slacks and a shirt.

The motor had been thoroughly checked in Lisbon. Water-cooled it would run forever at full throttle. An under-surface exhaust system cut noise to a minimum. The only control was the throttle. A sharp pull on the starting cord brought the motor to life. He killed it quickly. She helped him carry the gear into the kitchen and went into her bedroom.

He was taking the night glasses out of their case when a sound from outside startled him. He looked up to see Reidemeister's head thrust through the window.

The Baron wore a clean white suit and wide straw hat. His obliquely slanted eyes were curious.

"Good morning — may I come in?"

MacLaren heard the bedroom door being quietly closed.

"Sure," he said and opened the back door. He uncapped a bottle of beer, suddenly dry. "How the hell did you get in?"

The Baron wiped a chair seat with a lace-trimmed handkerchief.

"I have a key to the gates. I called but the noise of your motor obviously prevented you from hearing. I walked along the cliffs since I had to see you. The woods at this hour are exhilarating."

MacLaren tilted the bottle. With the thermometer up in the nineties, the statement was unlikely.

"What did you want to see me about?" he asked suspiciously.

The Baron poked his cane at the dinghy, tentatively.

"Then you *are* a fisherman, after all. I came to collect your passport. Your charming friend's still here I hope?" He raised his nose, sniffing the air like an old bird-dog.

Emma's door opened. She came into the kitchen, her eyes hostile. The Baron bowed politely and started to fan himself with his hat.

"What's my passport got to do with you?" MacLaren said doggedly.

The Baron's tongue clicked against his teeth.

"It's the law. I own this villa. As landlord I'm obliged to register the details of your passport at the Camara. Since the lady is leaving, hers does not matter. You *are* going to Spain, madame?"

"Just as soon as we're free," Emma said pointedly.

Reidemeister planted his cane firmly between his legs and leaned the last of his chins on the handle.

"Then perhaps you will allow me to accompany you. I have some shopping to do in Villa Real."

The question was aimed at MacLaren but Emma answered.

"I don't think you understand the situation, Baron Reidemeister."

The Baron's eyes were bright with interest. "No," he said hopefully.

Emma's hand flew to her throat. "Mr. MacLaren and I would prefer to be alone. We'll never see one another again after today."

The Baron's full mouth was sympathetic. "It is often better in such circumstances not to be alone — I speak from experience, madame."

MacLaren unstoppered the buoyancy tube valves. The dinghy collapsed in a hiss of escaping air. There was no point in refusing the Baron's request.

"She's a little bit upset," he said as easily as he could. "We'll be glad to give you a lift to Villa Real. Just let me get out of these things."

He changed shorts for slacks and a sleeveless shirt and returned to the kitchen. Emma's face was stony. He laid his passport on the Baron's knee.

"I'd like this back as soon as possible. I need it for changing travelers' checks."

The Baron's face grew serious at the mention of money.

"Of course — tomorrow without fail. We will leave it

at the Camara on our way out of town. Tell me — am I wrong or did you not say you were no fisherman?" He was looking at the dinghy with fresh curiosity.

MacLaren dragged the salt burn of tobacco deep into his chest. He settled for a completely new invention.

"That's right, I'm not. Can you think of a better way for anyone interested in land to prospect the coast-line?"

Reidemeister's chuckle started in his belly, agitated his shoulders and died in a wheeze. He tilted his head, looking narrowly at MacLaren.

"Profit from the errors of others. You're three years too late, Mr. MacLaren. Every meter of ocean frontage in the Algarve has already been explored from Sagres to the Spanish frontier. By boat — by car — mules, even by helicopter. I'm too fat for that sort of thing. I wait till newcomers realize that it's difficult for a for-eigner to do profitable business with a Portuguese. I've been here enough time to no longer be considered a foreigner."

Emma's voice was harshly under control. "You'll have a very happy relationship together, I'm sure. May we go now?"

The Baron spread his hands in a gesture of apology. They walked out into a heat that hit like a hammer. The Baron guided the car to the upper town. The Camara was housed in a blue-washed building with marble steps. The Baron got out, flourishing MacLaren's passport.

"Two minutes," he promised. He vanished into the cool, water-sprayed courtyard.

She snatched at the dashboard, turning off the volume control on the radio. Her mouth was hostile.

"You must be mad, having this fat fraud in the car. I made it easy for you to get out of. You seem determined to put yourself on show with him."

He flicked the radio on again. "That's right — that's exactly what I am doing. Santa Cruz is where I want to be identified with — and Santa Cruz is obviously the Baron."

She bit at her lower lip. "I think you're wrong. Stephen will think you're wrong."

He kept his eye on the courtyard.

"Your yeasty performances are beginning to bug me. I don't even care what you think — I'll do this my way. There's something else. I wouldn't want to have to tell your husband why — but in my book you're one hundred per cent phony."

She mangled the handkerchief in her lap before answering.

"Have you ever given me a chance to be anything else?"

The Baron was tapping his way down the steps.

"Remember your lines when we get to the frontier," MacLaren said quietly. "You'll have an appreciative audience."

The wide avenue ran parallel to the river. He stopped the Chrysler in front of the customs building. Through the closed gates was the slip to the waiting ferry. There was enough space on deck to house three cars, each perched precariously alongside the other. Beneath the wheelhouse was a cabin for pedestrian passengers. He wound his window down as far as it would go. Shading his eyes, he looked across the shimmering stretch of water. Spain was a distant straggle of buildings — vaguely forbidding in spite of the BIENVENIDO painted in letters six feet tall. There was a promise of strange rich smells in baked alleys, the secrecy of flowered court-yards hidden behind high blank walls. Above all, an in-transigent contempt for all things foreign.

Emma opened the dash compartment and collected a few belongings. She thrust these into her handbag and snapped the catch.

"Will you come as far as the ferry with me?" she asked in a low voice.

He shrugged. "Sure. Baron?"

The Baron had been sitting majestically aloof, his stumpy arms folded across his chest. He nodded at a waterfront café. "My shopping is soon done. I will wait for you there. Madame!" He made a flowery gesture in her direction and walked off.

MacLaren carried her bags into the customs building. The breeze off the river cooled his sweat-covered back. Two days of Portuguese sun had added a tinge of apricot to her face and arms. Her red-brown hair was bound in a silk scarf, tied French-fashion.

She walked over to the hatch in the wall and pushed her passport through for franking. The police official's eyes followed her curiously as she walked back to Mac-Laren.

The Canadian wiped his damp neck. A group of black-clad women with shopping baskets sat patiently awaiting the signal to board the ferry. He had a sudden impression of being ringed by an audience intent on drama.

She lifted her face. "I think you'd better kiss me. Everybody seems to expect it."

He leaned over her, smelling the sharp fragrance of her body. Her mouth sought his, her nails digging deep in his shoulder. She stepped out of the embrace and took off her dark glasses. Her eyes held his.

"Goodbye," she said. "And take care."

"I'll do that," he replied. "I ought to be hitting the island about four tomorrow morning."

The crowd sitting on the benches started to move outside. He walked as far as he could, to the end of the building. The ferry backed away from the slip to the excited bawling of deckhands. It swung into the stream and held a diagonal course for the Spanish shore. Her bright head scarf made it easy to distinguish Emma among the knot of people standing by the wheelhouse. Her back was firmly turned on Portugal.

The Baron was loitering in the shade of a tree, fanning himself contemplatively with his hat. He greeted MacLaren with delicate commiseration.

"Painful, these scenes, what?"

MacLaren balled his shoulders. "Especially to the ego. She's married."

The Baron linked his arm in MacLaren's. "Occasions like this argue the desirability of sex without any emotional involvement. A drink?"

They sat at a table overlooking the swiftly flowing river. Reidemeister turned away from his consideration of the opposite bank.

"Do you know Spain, Mr. MacLaren?"

The cold beer fogged the inside of the glass. MacLaren took a long pull at it.

"I covered a story in Madrid ten years ago. An English woman shot her boyfriend. He was Spanish. I wouldn't say I *know* it."

The Baron wiped the dribble of Madeira from the corner of his mouth.

"A cruel somber country. Where sores fester in the sun. I'm afraid I no longer have a stomach for either poverty or cruelty."

It was cool sitting here by the water. The dusty drive back offered no pleasure. But there was much to do before the dinghy was launched.

"I don't imagine those on the receiving end do either," he said. "I don't like seeing kids crippled and hungry any more than you do. But if I ever had to make the choice I'd sooner live under the Most Christian Gentleman's rule than Mao-tse-tung's. You're less likely to be eliminated on the pretext that your grandfather's grandfather knew who *his* grandfather was. The MacLaren political Manifesto, in brief. We'd better get going."

"How about Germans?" The Baron's voice squeaked.

MacLaren shoved his chair back. "Aren't you the obstinate one. How about 'em?"

Reidemeister's open mouth showed back teeth like gold nuggets. "German girls of good family. I repeat, I find you sympathetic. You need a companion. If the Rillington-Barker doesn't appeal to you, Helga Schmeisser might. She's twenty-two, dark and writes blank verse."

"I think I'd better take a little time to lick my wounds. I just remembered something — about my passport. It's just possible that I'll be going to Sagres tomorrow. If I do, I'll spend the day there and sleep at the *pousada*. You'd better hang on to my passport till I get back and collect it."

The Baron nodded. "*Erotic* blank verse," he promised.

MacLaren pushed the powerful sedan to the limits of safety on the road home. He dropped Reidemeister on the town square. It was almost noon as he crossed the narrow Roman Bridge. The flat rocks below were covered with wetwash. The women stood at their work knee-deep in the stream. Clothes dried bone-white on the wild cane growing down the banks. A couple of miles on, he turned onto the dirt track leading to the villa. He reversed the Chrysler through the gates and shot the bolts. The broad front of the car prevented anyone outside seeing onto the garden. He changed back to a pair of brief shorts and rubbed almond oil into his skin. Easy did it, the first few days. After lunch he could swim and sleep. Later he would go into town and fill the spare fuel can. He walked through the house, bombing each room with a D.D.T. solution. He shut the window in the room Emma had used, spraying the mosquitoes clinging to the curtains. He still tasted her mouth on his. Her eyelids had dropped as her head tilted back. But not fast enough to hide the look of triumph.

The heat gave him a constant thirst. He went into the kitchen. Knocking the cap off a bottle of beer, he carried it outside.

The garden wall that enclosed the wilderness of flowers topped his head by three feet. He made the tour of the house, trying all outside doors. As long as the Chrysler blocked the front gates, he was safe from peasants and tourists. He sprawled on the thick carpet of Bermuda grass and drank his beer. A column of ants marched down the kitchen wall and into a geranium bush. A piece of paper caught in the mauve blossoms took his eye. He reached for it. The torn strips were fresh and unstained by weather. Idly he started putting the bits together. The word PASSPORT was followed by three exclamation marks.

He put the paper to his nose. It smelled strongly of the scent Emma used. He rolled over on his back, the sun making kaleidoscopic patterns behind his closed eyelids. *Whose* passport needed remembering — her own? Ever since they'd boarded the bus for London Airport she'd known where to find whatever she needed at the drop of a hat. Money, passport and ticket, each had its proper place in the big snakeskin bag that was rarely out of her grasp. He had a sudden feeling that the note had referred to him. It must have been written before the telephone conversation with Venner. Because not long after she'd suggested that he take his passport with him. Having said it, she wouldn't be likely to remind herself again. He pressed the piece of paper into the earth.

Suppose you played it on the other keyboard. What if

Mrs. Venner was readying some unexpected sleigh ride
for him. How would she be thinking . . . her own position was impregnable. She'd be tucked up in bed, separated from the shot that killed her husband by a two-
mile stretch of water. Suppose she'd decided secretly
that Venner's production would fool neither the law
nor the insurance company unless she produced her
husband's murderer. He was tailor-made for the part.
She'd discover Venner's body and accuse him of murder.
He'd come back here to find the cops waiting, the dinghy and carbine already retrieved. There'd probably be
a confrontation at the frontier with Emma playing a
Bette Davis role. *I know him, yes. We were lovers.* She
had traveled to Portugal with him — one last effort to
make him understand their affair had reached the end
of the line. She had continued the journey to Spain
where a forgiving husband was waiting on the island.
The £4,500 in the bank in Los Gatos? She knew nothing
of it. Unless it had been her dead husband's intention
to solve their problem his own way — by trying to buy
off MacLaren.

He sat up, telling himself that this was craziness. He
was running a scrap of paper and the antics of a compulsive liar into a nightmare. Nevertheless there was a sense
of danger too tangible to ignore. Venner wanted a trial
run. A variation in the schedule might help resolve his
own doubt. He brushed the ants from his legs and went
into the house. He might as well eat lunch in town, fill
the spare drum of fuel at the same time.

Late morning shoppers crowded round the open-air
market. Small curs, lop-eared and corkscrewed-tailed,

fought over the scraps the butcher tossed through his metal fly screen. MacLaren had the fuel drum filled and walked across to the terrace bar. He was at the head of the steps before he saw the Lubbocks. He recognized the girl he had seen through Reidemeister's telescope. Her enormous breasts were confined in a red string halter. Her hair, the color of unraveled new rope, was parted in the center. She wore bullfighter's trousers and sandals with thongs.

The only free table was next to them. He sat down. Mrs. Lubbock's Medusa head was crowned with a relic of Hong Kong garden parties.

"Hello!" she fluted. "Here's Mr. MacLaren, dear," she informed her husband. Colonel Lubbock's starched eyes expressed nothing at all.

"I'd like you to meet my niece, Antonia Rillington-Barker. This is Mr. MacLaren, Antonia. He's a writer."

MacLaren nodded. Life with the Lubbocks was full of surprises. A little reserve leaked into his answer.

"Very resourceful of you to have found out my name."

Mrs. Lubbock peered under green-shaded lids. "Not really. We simply go to the Camara and ask. I understand you're Canadian?"

"That's right," he admitted.

Mrs. Lubbock hissed at the waiter, rearranging her face for MacLaren. "Won't you join us?"

"How do you know he's not really anti-social, Aunt Lorna?" the girl asked.

MacLaren's refusal was polite. "I guess not, thanks all the same. I'm just in for a quick bite, then back to swim."

Mrs. Lubbock swayed behind an arm still out-stretched in invitation.

"Alone? I understand that the female you were with last night has gone on."

The girl swept her hair back, displaying a cascade of silver chains dangling from each ear. She looked at Mac-Laren and laughed. The sound was loud and abrupt.

"Poor lamb! You mustn't be offended. You might even get your name in the *Anglo-Portuguese News.* Aunt Lorna writes our local column." She turned her powder-blue eyes on her aunt and laughed again.

Lubbock cleared his throat, enunciating as if he were still mess president.

"Another time, then, perhaps, I suppose you're fixed up and all that in the house. I feel a bit guilty about last night. Lorna and I were discussing it later. Should have known better than to leave you at the mercy of that fellow. A fascist, you know, hand-in-glove with all the wrong elements. No, I'm afraid Reidemeister's com-pletely unreliable. As for his morals, they're nonexist-ent."

Mrs. Lubbock quelled the girl's defiant giggle and smiled archly at MacLaren.

"We don't make a *business* of selling land. But there's always the temptation to help nice people find what they're looking for. We like to do it more or less on a friendly basis."

"Absolutely," said Lubbock. "No trouble at all. One doesn't want to see one's own kind gypped."

"Indeed not," Mrs. Lubbock said regally. "So far we've managed to maintain decent standards here, Mr.

MacLaren. An enclave of people who still care about that sort of thing. Certainly not the Reidemeisters of this world. I think you realize what I'm trying to say."

MacLaren's face was guileless. "Well, not exactly, no. You mean you think I'd be an asset to the neighborhood?"

The Colonel looked as if he were welcoming a subaltern to the regiment.

"No doubt of it. You don't command men, you know, without knowing their worth. Mutual respect's the answer. Buy on a rising market. It's a good life here in the winter. The sun always shines — we have our own small parties." He waved a hand largely. "And all that."

The girl sank the last of her Americano. "Run while you can," she advised in a clear voice. "They're offering you a fate worse than death."

MacLaren wiped his mouth and spoke clearly. "I'll tell you. I grew up in a farming community where people like you were a joke on radio. You ought to be stuffed and hung on a wall."

Mrs. Lubbock's chin lifted in amazement. "I *beg* your pardon?"

MacLaren shrugged. "You don't really want me to go into the department of fuller explanation, do you?"

Mrs. Lubbock's mouth trembled. "Are you going to sit there," she demanded of her husband, "while this creature insults me?"

The Colonel's eyes darted hopefully inside the bar. He leveled a finger at MacLaren.

"Now look here . . ." he began belligerently.

MacLaren cut him short. "Play it on the organ."

Mrs. Lubbock got to her feet. "I can promise you you'll regret this, Mr. MacLaren. Come, Antonia."

The girl stopped combing her hair with her fingers. She leaned over MacLaren's shoulder as she passed.

"It hasn't been done in years," she said confidentially. "I think you're gorgeous." She hurried after her aunt and uncle.

The Lubbocks walked down the steps, their faces tight and withdrawn. MacLaren looked after them. Chance had brought him to Santa Cruz, provided the physical setting necessary for this exploit. The interlude, half comical, half sinister, was an object lesson in where not to make a future. In the meantime he needed rest. The night ahead promised to be a long one.

A somnolence only broken by scampering lizards lay over the villa. He ran the car into the garden, chained and bolted the front gates. The bedroom floor was covered with the bodies of dead flies. He closed the shutters and stretched out on the bed. It was four o'clock when he awoke. He showered and began assembling his kit. The green canvas bag swallowed charts, binoculars, compass — the frogman's suit. He pushed a broad-bladed knife into his pocket. He left bag, dinghy and motor just inside the beach door. Back in the kitchen, he hacked a few rough sandwiches and filled two bottles with drinking water.

The police court, the Mission — the first meeting with Emma Venner — seemed to belong to another existence. Reality was waiting on a couple of hundred acres sticking out of the ocean thirty miles east.

He fastened all the shutters and windows, hid the

front-door key under a stone outside. He opened the
back door. The deserted beach was washed by the outgoing tide. He slid down, barefooted in fine warm
sand. It took two journeys to move his equipment to
the edge of the water. He loaded the dinghy and
mounted the motor. The raised bow bobbed gently as
he pushed the craft out in front of him. When the waves
lapped his thighs he hauled himself aboard. The flat-
bottomed boat rode light under his added weight. He
settled himself comfortably, sitting waist-high. The
motor caught first time. He opened the throttle and set
a southeasterly course. The hoop of beach receded rapidly. Ahead was a shimmer of sun and salt water. Beyond the pine-covered bluff on his right, the shoreline
curved to where Santa Cruz straggled on its three hills.
Sun touched the gilded belfry of the church in the upper
town. Holding the tiller with his elbow, he leveled the
binoculars at the Baron's house. The long picture window came into sharp focus. Fancy trained the telescope
there on the dinghy. He imagined Reidemeister, sweat-
ing a little, lips parted and knowing. He lifted a hand in
a self-conscious salute and opened the throttle.

His charts showed a dozen coast-guard stations between here and the frontier. The first part of his plotted
course took him well outside the three-mile limit. Nevertheless, trained men would still be keeping the dinghy
under observation. To confuse interest from the shore,
he had planned a combination of motor, drift and oar
work. If an official craft hailed him, he'd simply jettison
his charts and compass. The tale was foolproof. He was
a foreigner living in Santa Cruz. He liked underwater

swimming and had lost himself in unknown waters. The
nearer he came to nightfall and the mouth of the Guadiana, the nearer he came to a successful landing on the
island. The fishing fleets would be out on both sides of
the estuary. Ships laden with copper ore from the mines
at São Domingo would be steaming out on the ebb tide.
Running the passage from Portugal to Spain would be
relatively simple under cover of darkness. Chugging diesel motors would drown out the sound of his own tiny
unit. He intended to use his oars to cover the last stretch
to Santa Eulalia. Hauling on the tiller, he turned the
dinghy in her own length and headed due east.

Stephen Venner — Tuesday 7 July 1964

THE Avenida Generalissimo Franco sloped gently down from the Plaza Marques to the waterfront. A paved concourse that ran down its middle was thickly planted with jasmine, peonies and hibiscus. Here walked an ever-wheeling parade of men and women, their voices blending in a metallic murmur. Occasionally a horse-drawn barouche clattered into the square. Other than that, no vehicle moved. A blind lottery ticket seller sat on the curb. Face lifted to the night, he was croaking, "Para h– o — y!"

Venner's back was to the wall, his table in the shadow thrown by an enormous acacia. The Café El Rey faced the fountain. Spray sped from the mouth of four stone dolphins, a cool iridescent curtain protecting the terrace. The clientele of the café was solidly masculine. Heads turned lazily at the clicking of women's heels. Eyes assessed the passing women with an arrogant possessiveness. A rare smell hung in the watered air, compounded of Canary Isles tobacco, jasmine and the ammoniac reek from the neighboring alleys.

Sodium arcs blazed outside the bus terminal up on the Plaza Marques. The booking hall was a brilliantly lighted stage where the ubiquitous Civil Guard controlled passengers, pop vendors and shoeshine boys alike.

Venner's baggage was under his table. The black and gray suitcases he had bought in Seville — the brown paper package that never left his sight. He had chosen his clothes carefully. The sort of outfit that would make an impact on people's memory. Blazer, white shoes and trousers, a yachting cap and dark glasses. A glass of amontillado and a saucer of Tabasco-spiced mussels were untouched in front of him.

Next to the bus terminal, a baroque building rose between massive colonades. An illuminated strip on the roof spelled out BANCO PENINSULAR. Venner flipped the pages of his passport. The substitution of MacLaren's picture for his own was impeccable. The two halves of the embossment were in perfect alignment. He'd taken barbiturates shortly after leaving Victoria Station — slept through the Channel crossing. His passport had been retrieved as the express train barreled into the amethyst light flooding the western suburbs of Paris. A cab had rushed him to Orly Airport. He took his place in the queue boarding the Madrid plane, bareheaded and carrying his dark glasses. A cop's nicotine-stained fingers juggled the passport and exit card. The man's wrist flicked, there was the double-thud of the date stamp. An indifferent voice said thank you.

He lifted his glass, sipping the nutty wine and looking at the bus terminal again. The yellow-faced clock over the entrance said a quarter past ten. MacLaren would just about be putting out to sea. There was neither margin left for error nor reason for it. The one faint question mark was how much time Paragon Insurance would take to close its case. From what he had been able to glean, a month at best, six at the outside. Until then, the £4,500 he had transferred to the Banco Peninsular had to keep them both. There was no more. The mortgage on Heronscourt had dried out the well. Without him there, the practice would finally collapse. Revenue wouldn't even cover office salaries and the bank charges. Emma had to understand that an equal division of assets was out of the question. Establishing a new identity in a place like Rio de Janeiro would be an expensive business.

He put his passport away as a ship's siren sliced the night, mournful and insistent. An oil tanker backed out of its berth in the docks at the bottom of the Avenida Generalissimo Franco. Riding lights illuminated a snarl of fuel pipes snaking over the quayside. On the other side of the harbor, a maze of squalid shanties fronted beaches that would stay deserted till the return of the fishing fleet. The island of Santa Eulalia lay somewhere out in the indigo distance.

A stuttering roar invaded the Plaza Marques. A cumbersome bus turned the corner, a pall of diesel fumes attached to its rear. Action froze in the terminal, giving an impression of a film stopped to create effect. The bus doors opened and the bystanders came to life again. An assortment of riffraff barged about the baggage ports offering assistance. First out were two nuns, to be quickly enveloped by a group of waiting religious. The busload dispersed slowly, fanning into the surrounding streets and alleys.

He stood, screened by a hoarding, watching the main booking hall. Emma appeared carrying two suitcases that she checked at the baggage counter. She was alone. She walked out of the terminal like a woman who knew where she was going. He moved into the light as she neared the fountain, holding up his hand. She quickened her pace and came over. She sat down and tore the scarf from her head.

"Get me something to drink before I scream. That bus ride was really an experience."

She slid a cigarette from the pack, fiddling nervously with it till the waiter arrived. She drained her glass and answered his inquiry.

"He should land about four in the morning. He's counting on the trip taking six hours. It might be a little more or less depending on currents."

He pushed out a foot, moving the canvas holdall from under the table.

"We'll get somebody to go with you and collect your bags. You can check this at the same time."

She looked at the bag incuriously. "What's in it?"

"A change of clothing. It's just possible that Mac-Laren will have brought his passport. I'll hole the dinghy and swim ashore if he has. I can pick up the bag afterwards."

She slapped at a gnat on her arm. "He won't bring any passport. I can promise you that."

His face tightened. "Then I'll have to go to Santa Cruz and get it, won't I?"

She brooded over clasped hands. "Watch him, Stephen. He'll be here, that's for sure, but watch him."

She turned her head as the siren sounded again. The tanker's lights pinpointed the darkness near the harbor entrance.

He leaned across the table. "I'll do it tomorrow night. When he goes down to the beach to leave on his return trip. I don't want you to leave him alone — not even for a second."

She opened her eyes very wide. "And where are you going to be?"

"I've got business at the bank," he answered. "I won't be gone more than a couple of hours."

She gave him a long and appraising look. "We might as well have this absolutely clear. You say tomorrow night. I'm not staying on that island a minute after four o'clock. I'm going to be right here — where lots of people can see me."

Her voice and manner fanned a secret flicker of hatred. It was as well she would never know how slenderly suspended her own life was.

"You'd better go and collect the keys," he said.

Her lower lip curled and she yawned. "The sooner the better — where?"

He pointed across the street at an alley blocked to traffic. Halfway down, a lamp illuminated a balcony trailing creeper.

"Ask for Señor García — he speaks English. He's
supposed to have delivered some stores to the house.
Pay him. There's bound to be someone who'll give you
a hand with the bags. Find out about the island boat.
If it's still over there, we'll need transport."

She crossed the concourse, carrying the bag, indifferent to the gallantries from the benches. It was ten minutes before she showed again in the lighted doorway. A
teen-age boy followed her. They disappeared in the
direction of the bus terminal. Venner left some money
by his glass and walked up to meet them.

She looked as if something had unsettled her.

"It's you he wants to see, not me. As far as I can make
out, he acts as caretaker. You know the way they are
about dealing with women."

He took the baggage check she was offering. "Then
let's get a move on — what about the boat?"

She fell into step beside him. "It's still there. This
boy's going to ferry us over. You'd better see García
yourself otherwise you'll have him coming out to the
island. He wants to talk to you about the water supply."

"I'll telephone," he answered impatiently. "When
I'm here in the morning."

The boy unfastened his belt. Threading it through the
suitcase handles, he slung all four over his shoulder.

They followed him down the street, Venner carrying
the wrapped package himself. His reflection in the store
windows encouraged him. The raffish figure in yachting
cap and dark glasses would certainly be recognized in the
body on the beach.

The wine bars along the Embarcadero were loud with

guitar music. The boy led them away, past rows of ship chandlers' stores shuttered for the night. He crossed the street to the harbor wall. Steps were cut in the stone face. A small boat rode the faint swell ten feet below.

The boy grinned and gestured into the darkness. His teeth were brilliant. "Santa Eulalia." He lowered the bags into the boat, kicked off his shoes and started the motor. Venner gave his wife a steadying hand. They sat with their backs to the Spaniard, bilge slopping round their ankles. The boy stood at the tiller, singing the same catch repeatedly. It rose on six ascending notes, paused, his nose expelling the last lament.

They were well out, chugging into deep water. Emma moved her feet fastidiously. Venner's voice was curt.

"You're supposed to have come a thousand miles for a holiday. Try to look as though you're enjoying it."

He leaned into the slight pitch, intent on the vague shape that loomed in front of them. Another ten minutes brought them into the lee of the north shore of the island. Visibility was limited but he could have mapped Santa Eulalia accurately from memory. Its length ran roughly east to west. Rain-carved arroyos reached deep into the wooded slopes. The climb to the central plateau where the house lay was stepped with flat-topped pines.

They headed for a small rockbound beach. Winter gales had gouged tiny anchorages in the western promontory, digging out grottoes that would fill at high tide. The Spaniard cut his motor, letting the boat swing in towards an iron rail cemented in the stone above his head. He grabbed it and pulled the dinghy along the rockface into a small haven. A second boat covered with tarpaulin was tied to a small wooden pier. A short steel ladder linked the head of the pier to a path over the promontory. This in turn led into an arroyo at the back of the beach. The boy tied up alongside the pier and lifted out the suitcases.

Venner jumped out. "Get rid of him. We don't want him coming up to the house." He pulled on a pair of thin gloves. If the police ever decided to look for finger-prints, all they'd find would be Emma's and MacLaren's. He started up the ladder, carrying two of the bags. He heard his wife's halting Spanish, the boy's quick grati-tude. Emma handed up the other cases. By the time they reached the beach, the dinghy was out of sight. The sound of the boy's singing drifted back over the water.

There was a glimpse of a long low house through the trees above. It stood on the ledge of a red sandstone cliff. Their path merged into the bottom of the ravine. For-gotten rains had deposited lengths of cane, now brittle and sun-bleached. The fine sand ran from underneath their feet, making the going difficult. The steep sides of the arroyo were thickly carpeted with the fleshy fingers of mesembryanthemum. They had to climb over uptorn pines lying transversely across their path. Venner stopped for breath. A flight of brick-faced steps zigzagged round the oleanders overhead. They went up in Indian file, husbanding their wind.

The view from the summit was spectacular. The simple house was built on one level. A patch of burned grass extended from the front windows to the edge of the cliff. Fifty feet below, the ocean boomed in the cave fissures. He walked round to the back of the house. Starlight softened the ugly lines of a circular water cistern. Broom, gorse and cactus encroached on what had once been a garden. Three hundred yards or so distant, the silhouettes of umbrella pines marked the southern limit of the plateau. Beyond this was the beach where MacLaren would land.

He made his way round to the front again. Emma was sitting on one of the cases, staring at the mainland.

"You can't wait to get off again, can you?" he asked sourly.

She turned her head slowly. "Are you getting nervous, Stephen?"

He was first to break, taking his eyes from her smile. "Give me the keys."

The front door opened on a smell of fresh whitewash. Palm fronds in an earthenware jar drooped over a bare brick floor. He held a match high and walked through to the kitchen. Four lamps on the dresser were filled with pink kerosene. He lit them all. A couple of cartons of provisions were stacked on top of the gas refrigerator. The typewritten message in English was scotch-taped to the wall over the sink: EASY ON THE WATER IT'S A LONG WAY TO THE WELL.

He carried one of the lamps into the other room. The furniture was Barcelona, circa 1928. Mosquitoes whined in the folds of the curtains. There were a few highly colored religious pictures and a view of Granada taken from the air.

He dumped their bags in the kitchen. Emma was sitting by the refrigerator.

"We're not expected to sit up waiting for him. He said he'd sleep on the beach till six or seven. I've had a long day. I think I'll go to bed."

He hoisted the brown paper package onto the table. "Everybody's had a long day. This'll be our last chance to tie up any loose ends."

She leaned back against the wall, her eyes smudged with fatigue. "Not again — My part of it's crystal-clear."

He snapped the cord with gloved fingers and lifted out the shotgun. The barrels had been sawn off six inches away from the stock. He clocked the hammers on an empty breach.

"This took me two sets of hacksaw blades and the better part of yesterday evening. It's secondhand, Spanish and absolutely untraceable." He pushed a couple of twelve-bore cartridges into the breach. The business end of the weapon pointed at her stomach.

Smoke curled past her narrowed eyes. "Isn't that rather drastic for cigarette smugglers?"

His grip eased on the stock. He thumbed up the safety catch. "He'll never know what hit him. Anyone with four thousand pesetas could have bought this thing and modified it. I've filed off all identifying marks. By the time the police get busy with the clues I leave for them, every smuggler between here and Algeciras will be on the run."

She cocked her head, eyes puzzled. "What's that noise? Like someone coughing."

He listened and heard nothing. "A goat or a sheep, probably. Now remember, you'll be alone with Mac-

Laren tomorrow morning while I go into the bank.
Whatever you do, keep him occupied. He might want to
sleep again. If he does, stay near him."

"Suppose the bank decides you don't look like the
picture on your passport — there's always the first time."

He opened his briefcase. The bank draft and covering
letter were issued from Zurich.

"The people here already have a copy of this letter.
You can see if you look — the number of my passport
is already quoted for identification purposes. I'm going
to leave this place ransacked. Even a policeman will find
it hard to avoid the logic. Whoever blew my head off
stole the money."

She read the letter thoroughly. "What about my share,
Stephen?"

"As far as the authorities are concerned, you never
knew this cash existed," he said easily. "Address yours
to yourself at some Poste Restante address. And have a
story ready to account for being in possession of a thousand pounds' worth of pesetas, just in case."

She covered her temples with her hands. "A thousand
pounds worth! Something's happened to your arith-
metic."

He ran himself a glass of water and added a purifying
tablet. She'd learn.

"I don't think so. You're going back to Kingston Hill
not Brazil. For the moment our requirements are different."

Her eyes appraised him. She was tapping the top of
the refrigerator with outstretched fingers.

"An understatement if ever there was one. I want to

know what I'm meant to say when the insurance company people come to see me. They'll have found out about the money you owe the bank — all the other debts. Am I supposed to play the innocent or what?"

Some feat, he told himself. He shook his head.

"Just treat it as a matter of course. Naturally we've got debts. Who hasn't in our class? Half the professional people in England are in the same boat. That doesn't mean they go around plotting their own death. Try to get this into your head, Emma — a murdered man is the *victim* of a crime not its perpetrator."

She seemed to be doodling on the back of an envelope.

"Are you listening to what I'm saying?" he asked sharply.

"I'm listening," she said calmly. She brought the envelope up in front of her chest so that it was hidden from the window.

He read the lipstick scrawl: SOMEONE OUTSIDE.

He moved rapidly, burning his hands on the lamp funnels in his haste to extinguish the lights. He threw the door open. He had a quick glimpse of MacLaren's back, then the Canadian crashed into the bush twenty yards away. Venner caught his wife's arm, pushing a taut accusing face into hers.

"Four o'clock in the morning?"

She wrestled free and dashed inside. By the time he reached the kitchen, she already had one of her suitcases open. She exchanged her dress for trousers, moving speedily but without panic.

"Get those things off," she instructed. "Put on something dark."

He grabbed blue slacks and a dark gray cardigan. He pushed himself into them mechanically, repeating the same thing over and over — as if repetition would bring meaning to the whole thing.

"Four o'clock in the morning!" His hands had started to shake.

She tied a scarf round her hair, crossed the room and took him by the shoulders. Strong fingers held him firmly.

"Make an effort, Stephen. We're finished unless you get a grip on yourself. Do you understand?"

He wet his mouth and nodded. "He heard—of course he heard."

"All he needed," she answered. "We've got to stop him getting off the island. I'm going down to the landing stage. You look for his dinghy and put it out of action."

She picked the shotgun from the table and stuffed a handful of spare shells into her trouser pocket. He watched, fascinated, as she thumbed up the safety catch and cocked both hammers. He heard his voice break a little.

"You'll blow yourself to bits like that."

Her features hardened into an expressionless mask.

"It's not the moment for advanced lessons. I know how to pull a trigger. That's enough."

He tucked his shirt collar into the cardigan. He was glad she was there to think for him.

"Suppose he's armed himself?"

She pointed impatiently at his unlaced sneakers. "He isn't. I searched his bags twice *and* his clothes. A fisherman's knife, that's all he's got. Just keep out of his way.

You're concerned with the dinghy. Let me take care
of him."

He looked up from a kneeling position. "I have to
know what I'm doing, Emma. What you're going to do."

Her eyes were implacable. "What do *you* think. He'll
be safe enough in the house until I get to the mainland.
Then it's up to you."

He lumbered to his feet and opened the back door.
He took the shortcut across the plateau, kicking his way
out of the thorn that tore at his legs. A strong rank smell
hit his nostrils. At the same time, a flock of sheep can-
tered into the clearing, terrified and bleating. They came
off a track in the woods to his left. He pictured Mac-
Laren waiting in the trees, a knife in his hand.

The entrance to the southern arroyo was in front of
him. He slid down into shifting sand, leaping roots and
stumbling out of rabbit warrens. Suddenly the ocean
was there before him. The creamy wash of the incoming
tide was already three parts up the beach. He stopped
to get his bearings. There was no sign of the dinghy but
the hiding places were limited. The beach was a hundred
and fifty yards long, running between a couple of volcanic promontories. The pines here along the foreshore
were sparser than those up on the heights. Erosion had
left most of them with bleached, exposed roots. He
trotted from one tree to the other exploring any aper-
ture that was large enough to contain MacLaren's boat.
A thorough search of the gorse and oleander proved
equally useless. The sand showed no trace of anything
having been hauled out of the water.

He looked nervously up the slope. A tic had started

under his left eye. He brushed at it vaguely. MacLaren
would be aware now of two things — that his presence
on the island was known — that he'd die if he didn't get
off it. But suppose the dinghy had drifted or been holed
on the rocks in landing. MacLaren was fit and his brain
worked fast. The whole pattern of the Canadian's thinking made an open attack by him likely — even with
nothing more lethal than a bait knife. He had two hundred acres in which to maneuver and five hours till
dawn. Daylight was his enemy. He must aim now at
what he thought the weakest point in the closing ring.

Venner had a vivid impression of being hunted himself — as if he were the quarry and not MacLaren. Instinct told him the other man was not far away—
possibly watching him at this very moment. He had a
sudden desire to be with Emma, standing on the right
end of the shotgun. He climbed out of the arroyo and
stood for a moment listening. Something or someone
had disturbed the sheep again. They were thudding
about on the far side of the plateau. He went into his
ungainly dogtrot, lifting his knees in exaggerated fashion. He kept well clear of the dark green vault on his
right. Imagination produced a figure that ran there in
time with him, crouching low and menacing.

He needed speed rather than silence and forced flag-
ging muscles till they refused duty. He half fell into
the northern ravine and stumbled down the path to the
landing stage. Fear put caution back into his head.
Where the path narrowed, hugging the cliff face, he stole
forward quietly. Moving his head warily, he looked over
the top of the steel ladder. The island boat was knocking

against the wooden pier with dull insistence. He cupped
his hands round his mouth and directed the loud whisper down into the tiny harbor.

"Emma!"

He expected her to come from the shadows beneath
the overhang. Nothing moved. He lowered himself
down the ladder and lifted the tarpaulin that covered
the boat. The oars were missing. Someone had removed
the spark plug from the motor. A pebble ricocheted off
the rock, struck the edge of the jetty and plopped into
the water. He dropped the tarpaulin as if discovering
it to be alive and dangerous. He raised his head sharply,
staring up at the overhang.

"Emma?" he repeated, then softened his tone cunningly. "MacLaren — don't be a fool, MacLaren — we
can talk this out between us."

A hoopoe called, plaintive in a tree up by the house.
He took a pace backwards, unnerved more than anything by not being able to locate MacLaren. He and
Emma should never have separated. He thought briefly
of taking refuge in the boat, then remembered that she
had put it out of commission. He started up the ladder,
flinching from whatever waited for him at the top.
Once up on the path, he put his head down and ran. The
deep soft beach sand slowed him down to an unbalanced
lope. He fell to his knees twice, rising like an animal
momentarily creased by a spent bullet.

He approached the house apprehensively, using the
water tower as cover. The lights were still out, the
kitchen door wide open. There was the brooding silence
of a house left empty. The bleating sheep stampeded

back into his thoughts. It was Emma they had been running from — not MacLaren. She must have come through the woods, looking for him. He would have passed her on the way without knowing it. He found himself making decisions and discarding them as quickly.

He pictured MacLaren sitting in the darkened house, the broad-bladed knife open and ready. His hands were opening and shutting on air. He throttled the cough that crept treacherously into his throat. As far as Emma knew MacLaren's dinghy was on the south shore. Almost certainly she would have gone in that direction. But what if he missed her again . . . anything was better than what he was doing to himself.

He inched away from the water tower and made his way round to the front of the house. The shutters were still closed. He flattened himself against the wall, his sneakers soundless on the dry Bermuda grass. He sidled towards the front door. It stood ajar. He reached with a hand and gave it a tentative shove. His ears strained for any sound to be construed as danger. Only the palm fronds shivered in the slight breeze through the open door. He took three steps forward into the hall. A flash came from the left-hand bedroom, the explosion shattering his eardrums. He rose high on his toes, clutching at what was left of his chest. In the second between life and death he seemed to hear his wife's cry of alarm. Then, spinning round, he fell heavily onto his face.

Ross MacLaren — Wednesday 8 July 1964

THE shot came from the direction of the house. The noise echoed from one side of the island to the other in a series of ever-diminishing explosions. He was laying across the fork of a tree, the scabby bark scoring his bare arms. He lifted his head a few inches, looking up through the green tracery. A thousand stars were nailed against an indigo sky. The long white house on the plateau glimmered in the reflected light, enigmatical in the ensuing hush.

He had tailed Venner to the south shore and watched the lawyer's fruitless search of the beach. The dinghy was concealed in a cove two hundred yards beyond the western promontory. Without help of daylight the Venners had no hope of locating his hiding place for it. He had slipped round behind the lawyer, aiming for higher ground. From there he could outflank the man and scale the rocks down to the dinghy. The second stampede of sheep sent him headlong into the bushes bordering the stand of pines. Dust from the animals' hoofs hung in the still air, obscuring the view at ground level. It settled after a couple of seconds. He lay there, his heart a hammer in his chest. He concentrated on the spot where the sheep track that ran through the woods came to an end. There was a faint rustle — an impression of an oval paler than the surrounding shadows.

She broke cover stealthily, her head a little raised as if she sensed his nearness. She was carrying the shotgun at port, the stubby sawed-off barrels flicking from side to side like a snake's tongue. He kept quite still, his cheek pressed into the pungency of thyme. She ran across the plateau, lightly and determinedly. From the angle at which he lay it was impossible to track her beyond the water cistern on the skyline. She might have forked right and into the house through the back or left in the direction of his cove. Shortly after, Venner had charged up the arroyo, arms pumping — sweaty-faced and breathing painfully. He was almost near enough to touch. MacLaren had followed the lawyer as far as the landing stage, retreating back to the woods when his foot dislodged the pebble. Minutes later the shot disturbed the night.

He moved now in the fork of the pine, taking hold of a branch. He swung out and down, dropping ankle-deep in needles. The silver light radiating behind the summit threw a geometrical pattern of shade around the house. He placed at least one of them inside the building. Unless the weapon had changed hands, it had to be Emma. Nerves or bluff could have touched off the shot he had heard. He worked his way cautiously to the perimeter of the thicket. A deep sense of outrage blunted his fear. That his death had been determined the day Emma picked him up in the mission was temporarily forgotten. What needled was the fact that he'd been the mark in about the brassiest con of all time. Steered from one Venner to the other like a country boy in the hands of a couple of operators.

He watched the blank shuttered windows up above. As if on cue Emma came through the kitchen door. She moved more slowly than before, heading for the far side of the plateau. His guess at the reason for the shot now seemed a probable one. Alone in the house she had heard some sound and fired instinctively. He fancied her crouched against a wall in the darkness, her ears and nostrils filled with the blast. Panic would do the rest. Venner must have made his way back across the island. She would run for the south beach and her husband.

Keeping to the shelter of the trees, he started to move north, away from her measured walk. He hit the brick-faced path from the landing stage to the house about halfway up. Far across the water, signals blinked at the entrance to Los Gatos harbor. Beyond that blazed the lights of the town. A town that as far as he was concerned could be a thousand miles away. His plan was simple. To follow the sheep tracks hammered along the contours of the cliffs. These cut through the woods only when there was no alternative. The cove where his dinghy was hidden lay five hundred yards in a straight line across the island. The way he had chosen obliged him to cover six times this distance. But it offered the sea as a constant refuge.

He took the last few steps towards the house at a run. The ground under the wiry Bermuda grass was hard with the stored heat of the day. He went silently past the shut-tered windows, alert to any possible indication of dan-ger. The open front door shivered an inch in the breeze lifting off the sea. A booming roar sounded in a blowhole in the rocks deep below. He stopped opposite the door, his body stiff with apprehension. A dark pool spread across the stone step. The smell of blood was unmistak-able. He traced the liquid streak across the hall and then moved fast, instinct and training combining in self-preservation. Ripping off his shirt, he tore it into gaunt-lets for his hands. He came into the hall, adjusting his eyes to the diminished light. He stepped carefully, avoiding the stains on the tiles. He bent over the body.

Venner was laying face down, his arms outstretched. His hands were resting on the wall, the nails broken and scarred with whitewash. The charge had obviously been fired from a sitting position. A chair was just inside the open door to the bedroom. The shell had taken the law-yer high on the pectoral, blasting away part of his thorax. The ruptured throat artery would have leaked life away in a matter of seconds.

A faucet was dripping in the kitchen. MacLaren put his head over the sink, letting the tepid water run on his neck. Still fighting his nausea, he went through the papers in Venner's briefcase. They were self-explanatory.

The Paragon policy insuring Venner's life for a hun-dred thousand pounds. A receipt for dental work done for Mr. Stephen Venner. A car-hire bill in the same name. He opened the lawyer's passport, certain whose picture he would find there. He dropped the passport on the floor. Holding a match clumsily with his shrouded hands, he set fire to the document. He scooped up the ashes and scattered them outside the kitchen door. There was a strange sense of finality about it all — as if this and nothing else had been ordained by the Fate Sisters. Venner was dead. The only thing left now was to determine his killer.

He turned back on his tracks, following the arroyo down to the north beach. The landing stage was empty, the island boat still swinging lazily from its painter. He lowered himself down the ladder and clambered aboard. Unshipping the metal tiller, he smashed a hole well below the waterline. He jumped back onto the landing stage as the boat started to founder. It sank in seconds. He stood, looking down through the clear water. The boat lay on the ocean bed, the tarpaulin lifting slightly in the current.

He wiped his face and neck with his cloth-covered hands and hauled himself up to the path. This time he made a detour round the house, all his senses projected in an attempt to locate the woman. The issue lay between them now. He had no illusion about her intentions. She was too smart to have deliberately shot her husband. Too much aware of the hopelessness of her position. She was quick like a fox, though, and desperate now. If she winged or maimed him — killed even — there was still a chance to act out some story that would clear her. But she was a goner once he was off the island. His tracks had been too well covered by them all. He could never be more than a wraith in the imagination of a woman who killed for profit. Once he was off the island, she would think again. And again. Till finally she broke and made her confession.

The sheep track led him high along the edge of the cliffs, through clumps of sweet-smelling bush, over dried-up patches of pasture dotted with dung. The southern exposure sloped away sharply, thickly planted with the ubiquitous umbrella pine. Overhead the stars were brilliant. He checked his watch. A quarter to one. There were still hours of darkness left for the trip back to Portugal. He recognized the outline of the promontory ahead. A rough shape of a bird etched in volcanic rock. He slowed to a walk, seeing the cove beneath. He could just make out the lines of the dinghy, thirty feet below.

The first half of the way down was over terraces of sandstone. He unwrapped his fingers, throwing the rags into the water. He was halfway down to the first tier of stone when the shotgun roared from the trees behind him. Slugs spattered the rock, whining in the air like outsize mosquitoes. If he stayed below her line of fire he was finished. He ran for the overhanging bushes. Reaching up he dug his fingers deep in tangled roots. Sand sifted into his eyes. A bush tore loose as he switched handhold. For a second he was suspended in space. He grabbed again, using forearms and knees in an effort to gain fresh purchase. The maneuver brought his head and shoulders above solid ground, thirty yards away from her. It was near enough to hear the click of her reloading. He started running again, jinking and leaping the fissures that weakened the cliff structure. Roots grabbed at his heels. He half slid, half fell, into a fault

in the ground covered with weeds. He clawed vainly,
his legs thrashing to find bottom. He dropped suddenly,
a long way down to a stone floor. A shower of stones followed.

He heard the sound of her pursuit slow to a walk —
then stop. Dirt cascaded down on his head. He looked
up. The shotgun barrels were being pushed through the
grass down into the hole. He was blocking the narrow
fissure with his shoulders. There was plenty room for
him to stand upright. He could go forward or backward
but not sideways. She had slanted the snout of the shotgun behind him. He shuffled ahead, hands outstretched
— seeker in some deadly game of blind man's buff. He
passed directly under the crack of light.

The sudden nearness of her voice startled him. She
was either lying flat on the ground or kneeling.

"I can see the bottom from here — you'll never get out
without help."

He raised his eyes. The stone ceiling was cowl-shaped.
He had dropped through the hole at its apex. He was at
least fifteen feet below surface with no hand-holds anywhere in the smooth rock. He shuffled a few more steps
forward. Her voice followed, muffled and coaxing.

"I don't want to face this alone — I need help. Trust
me, Ross. If I really wanted to hurt you, all I have to do
is walk away and leave you here."

A silence.

"Don't you see that, Ross?"

The top of his head struck against the sloping ceiling. The walls narrowed at the same time as the roof
dropped. The passage was now no larger than a sewerage

pipe. He went into it, propelling himself with knees and stomach. There was a complete absence of light now. The faintness of her voice completed the impression of a great distance between them.

"I'm going to lower my belt," she was saying. "Then you can . . ."

He lost the rest of it in the scraping of his toes against the rock. In spite of the drop in temperature, he had started to sweat. An immense weight seemed to be pressing his head down. Fear of meeting a blank wall accompanied each inch he gained. Worst was the knowledge that if ever the passage did come to an end he would have to return backwards.

He pulled himself forward, his fingers feeling along the base of the walls. The passage suddenly became more spacious. This time it was his forehead that thudded against stone. He lay with his arms spread wide, cool air blowing on each hand. He brought them slowly together. Rock prevented them from touching.

He realized that the passage had divided in two. The stream of air was no stronger in one than the other. He shut his eyes, trying to reorient himself. The cliff he'd scaled — the terraced boulders leading down to the cove — these had to be on his right. The new passage he chose was no wider than the first. But after a dozen yards he could see light. The feeling of weight lifted from his head. He found he could stand. He lifted his eyes at the patch of sky above, seeing the familiar outline with disbelief. Darkness and confinement had tricked his sense of direction. What he was looking at was the hole by which he had entered.

He had an urge to shout—to bring her running
with a rope or something. Who cared what came next.
Better take a chance with a twelve-bore than die like a
bug in a bottle. Hope dragged back into his thinking.
He started to return the way he had gone before. It was
easier this time, till he reached the fork in the tunnel at
least — then every nerve fought his brain in rebellion.
Steady streams of sweat ran into his eyes. His skin
scraped and chafed beyond pain. He knew vaguely that
he was saying the same words over, encouraging
himself to go forward. The passage was serpentine,
each bend at once a threat and a promise. He seemed to
have covered a hundred yards when his fingers touched
slime. He fumbled blindly, using his nose to identify
the mess as bird droppings. Then the current of air was
salt on his lips. A few more yards and he saw light again,
this time at body level. He crawled the last few feet and
straightened up.

He was in a small cave gouged in the side of the volcanic promontory. A thin finger of rock separated the
water below from his cove. He dropped ten feet into
the warm sea. His breast stroke barely disturbed the
surface. He rounded the point, avoiding the razor-edged
rocks spiking the mouth of the cove. He covered the last
few yards to the dinghy at a fast crawl and pulled himself
aboard.

A slash of the bait knife freed the painter. Perched
on his knees, he pulled the starting cord. The motor fired
once and then stalled. The small craft rocked under his
weight. The dying splutter of the motor echoed in the
cove. Then a voice called. She was almost directly above

him. Her face in the starlight reflected off the water seemed part of the stone she was standing on. He whipped the starting cord frantically as she lifted the shotgun. The motor caught and he gunned it. He crouched low, swinging the tiller from side to side. The dinghy roared seaward. Her last shot plowed the surface of the ocean twenty feet behind him.

When he looked back, the place where she had been standing was empty. Whether she'd chosen land or water he'd never know. Taking a fresh hold on the tiller and sitting up, he aimed the dinghy at the mouth of the river and Portugal.